"In a perfect world I'd go lock that door and make love to you," Trip said.

"Would I have any say in it?" she asked.

"Absolutely."

"Well, then, in a perfect world, I'd race you to the door to see who got there first to turn the lock."

Faith looked surprised by her own words. Before she could take them back, he touched her lips with his own. Holding the sides of her head, her hair like silk beneath his fingers, he gently kissed every part of her face he could reach.

She returned the favor, her warm, wet mouth awakening every corpuscle in his body. He wanted to peel her out of her clothes as she grew softer and warmer with each passing second.

Suddenly, she twisted away from him. Her breathing sounded labored as she rested her forehead against his shoulder. "It's not a perfect world," she murmured, reminding him of the danger that lurked right outside their door.

Trip ran his fingers down a strand of her golden hair and whispered, "I noticed."

ALICE SHARPE

AGENT DADDY

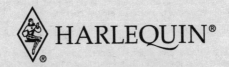

HARLEQUIN®

TORONTO • NEW YORK • LONDON
AMSTERDAM • PARIS • SYDNEY • HAMBURG
STOCKHOLM • ATHENS • TOKYO • MILAN • MADRID
PRAGUE • WARSAW • BUDAPEST • AUCKLAND

This book is dedicated to my beautiful mother,
Mary Rose LeVelle, who has always been there for me.

Recycling programs
for this product may
not exist in your area.

ISBN-13: 978-0-373-88940-2

AGENT DADDY

Copyright © 2009 by Alice Sharpe

www.eHarlequin.com

Printed in U.S.A.

ABOUT THE AUTHOR

Alice Sharpe met her husband-to-be on a cold, foggy beach in Northern California. One year later they were married. Their union has survived the rearing of two children, a handful of earthquakes registering over 6.5, numerous cats and a few special dogs, the latest of which is a yellow Lab named Annie Rose. Alice and her husband now live in a small rural town in Oregon, where she devotes the majority of her time to pursuing her second love, writing.

Alice loves to hear from readers. You can write her at P.O. Box 755, Brownsville, OR 97327. SASE for reply is appreciated.

Books by Alice Sharpe

HARLEQUIN INTRIGUE

746—FOR THE SAKE OF THEIR BABY
823—UNDERCOVER BABIES
923—MY SISTER, MYSELF*
929—DUPLICATE DAUGHTER*
1022—ROYAL HEIR
1051—AVENGING ANGEL
1076—THE LAWMAN'S SECRET SON**
1082—BODYGUARD FATHER**
1124—MULTIPLES MYSTERY
1165—AGENT DADDY

*Dead Ringer
**Skye Brother Babies

CAST OF CHARACTERS

Luke Tripper—Once an FBI agent, "Trip" is now a reluctant rancher and "Daddy" to his orphaned niece and nephew. He'll do whatever it takes to protect those he loves from the violence of his past.

Faith Bishop—Still recovering from injuries sustained back in her hometown, she's moved to Shay for solitude and quiet. What she's found is terror and danger—and maybe the love of her life.

Gina Cooke—The babysitter for Trip's niece and nephew. Her mysterious disappearance sets everything in motion. Is she alive or is she dead? Who's responsible?

David Lee—Is this bodybuilder content to bully Faith or is he out for blood?

Neil Roberts—An escaped serial killer with one thing on his mind—destroy the man who sent him to prison (and anyone else who gets in the way).

Eddie Reed—What secrets does his shy manner mask? Will this mechanic come through when all else fails?

Peter Saks—Gina's boyfriend has a major attitude problem. He claims he loved Gina—did he love her to death?

Police Chief Thomas Novak—This lawman doesn't appreciate Trip's experience. Is there more to his bluster than meets the eye?

Chapter One

Thanks to the fussy baby in the backseat and the rain pounding the truck cab, it was amazing Luke Tripper heard the shrill ring of his cell phone. He answered quickly, expecting to hear his foreman detailing yet another problem on the ranch. "Trip here."

The response was a gravelly voice Trip had assigned to his past. "What's that racket?" his former boss demanded. Timothy Colby was the SAC of the Miami office of the FBI and he had the bark to prove it.

A quick glance in the rearview mirror revealed tufts of reddish-blond hair, eyes squeezed almost shut, plump, tear-stained cheeks and two new teeth that glowed like freshwater pearls. "That noise is a frustrated ten-month-old baby," Trip said.

"Say again? I can barely hear you."

"It's Colin, my nephew," Trip all but yelled. His raised voice did what his cajoling murmurs hadn't been able to—Colin abruptly stopped crying. Into the relative quiet, Trip added, "What can I do for you, Mr. Colby?"

"Miss the Bureau yet?"

"I haven't had time," Trip replied.

"I thought being knee-deep in babies and cows, you might miss the excitement, the danger—"

"If you think infiltrating a group of terrorists is tricky, you've haven't tried to raise two little kids," Trip said. "And please, don't get me started on ranching."

Colby laughed, or maybe he growled. The exact spirit of the noise was hard to define.

A car in the other lane swerved too close and Trip accelerated out of the way. He'd witnessed a terrible accident on this very road just a few months before, when a bus driver suffered a heart attack and the bus careened off the highway. He had no intention of being part of one now. "Sir, I'm running late. If this is a social call, maybe I could get back to you later."

"Not just social," Colby said, his voice sobering. "It's about Neil Roberts."

Trip frowned. "What about him? He's rotting away in jail."

"No. He got away during a prison transfer last night. Killed an officer in the process. Given your past relationship with this man, I wanted to give you a heads-up."

Special Agent in Charge Timothy Colby wasn't the kind to overreact. The fact he felt it prudent to issue a warning went a long way with Trip. "Is there any word Roberts is headed in this direction?"

"Not exactly, but he escaped on his way to Pelican Bay Penitentiary, down in California. All that stands between you and him is the state of Oregon."

Trip glanced back at his nephew again. The baby had snagged Trip's beloved Stetson and was putting his new teeth to work gnawing on the brim. "What are you doing to get him back?"

Colby detailed the combined police and FBI efforts to recapture Roberts and promised to stay in touch. They disconnected just as Trip took the exit into Shay.

The grammar school was on the other side of town and traffic was a mess—made more harrowing by frantic Christmas shoppers with less than two weeks left. Trip drove with extra caution, knowing he was distracted by Colby's news.

Neil Roberts on the loose. Neil Roberts, the scum of the earth, the sludge beneath the mud. Trip didn't want the brute within a thousand miles of his niece and nephew, or anyone else for that matter.

Another glance in the rearview mirror revealed Colin had dropped the hat and was revving up for a new tirade. Not only was Trip running late, he was bringing a sibling to a meeting with his niece's new teacher—even Trip knew that was bad form. There wasn't a thing he could do about it, since the babysitter hadn't shown up or answered her phone. He'd kept his eyes peeled for her broken-down heap beside the road as he drove into town, but he hadn't seen it.

He pulled into the parking lot twenty minutes late, grabbed his hat and the baby and dashed through the rain to the front office. A few minutes later he had a visitor's pass and directions to the afternoon kindergarten. Happy to be out of the car seat, Colin hung on to Trip's collar, his small legs clenched tight around Trip's torso, making little excited noises as they hurried.

The kindergarten was off by itself at the end of a long hall. When Trip finally reached the door, he paused to catch his breath and peer into the classroom.

This close to Christmas break, the room was festooned with chains of colored paper and hanging snowflakes. Toy-cluttered shelves rimmed the perimeters, easels stood ready for young Picassos. Children's books were scattered across a circular rug in the middle of the room, and a fuzz ball in a cage next to the window gave a small exercise wheel a workout.

No teacher, no Noelle. Now what?

Part of him wanted to slink away. He was sure the teacher would have "suggestions" to fix whatever she thought he was doing wrong with Noelle, and he was just as sure he didn't want to hear them. This was a new teacher, barely here two weeks, a replacement for the last teacher who had left when her husband fell ill. That teacher had bombarded him with unsolicited advice.

Colin grabbed at a painting pinned to the wall and ripped off a corner, stuffing it into his mouth with lightning speed. As Trip rescued the rest of the painting from sure destruction and pried the paper out of Colin's mouth, the baby squealed—he might be small, but he had a mind of his own and the lungs to back it up.

At the sound of Colin's cry, Trip detected movement in the back of the room and watched as a woman seated at a desk he hadn't noticed before raised her head from her folded arms. She looked around blankly, blinking a few times until her gaze fastened on him and Colin. Like a shot, she was on her feet, speaking before she'd taken a step, straightening her ruffled white blouse, patting her hair, smiling.

"Mr. Tripper? Hello, welcome, I'm Ms. Bishop—Faith Bishop. I'm sorry, I…well, it looks like I nodded off."

At the sound of her voice, Colin swiveled in Trip's arms to face her, his noisy protest dissolving into a drooly grin and a series of coos.

At six foot three inches, Trip was used to towering over people, but this woman was truly petite, small-boned and delicate. She had a heart-shaped face, clear blue eyes, a delicate nose and surprisingly full lips. Wavy tendrils of wheat-blond hair escaped a little knot at the nape of her neck. Tiny silver earrings, no ring on any finger, slim hands, silver watch. He detected a slight limp, barely noticeable. He placed her in her midtwenties.

As she neared, the overhead fluorescent lights illuminated three or four fading scars on the left side of her face. He realized he'd been staring when her hand flew to her cheek, fingers barely grazing the scars before continuing on to push a few strands of hair behind her ear. It looked like a subconscious and recurring gesture.

Meanwhile, Colin was becoming increasingly hard to keep hold of, as he wiggled and kicked and stretched tiny arms toward the teacher. The cries morphed into squeaks of delight and anticipation as she stopped a foot or so away.

"You have to be Colin," she said to the baby. "Your big sister told me all about you."

Trip wondered what else Noelle talked about.

She was pretty quiet around him, though he was beginning to sense a slight thaw.

The woman took the baby's hands in hers and smiled up at Trip. "It's very nice to meet you, too. Thank you for coming in."

Colin had almost squirmed his way into her arms by now, and laughing, she took his weight. "Persistent little guy, isn't he?"

"You have no idea." Taking off his hat and running his fingers through his short hair, he added, "I'm sorry we're late. The babysitter didn't show up."

"Oh, that's okay," she said as she gently disengaged Colin's hands from her hair. She peeled the baby's damp jacket off of him and dropped it on a pint-size chair.

"She's usually pretty conscientious," he added, determining at that moment to swing by Gina's place on the way home and make sure she hadn't taken ill. "I know I'm not supposed to bring another child to a meeting, either, but there wasn't a choice."

"It's not a problem," she said. "Let's go back to my desk and talk about Noelle." Effortlessly hitching Colin on her right hip, she led the way to her desk. For a small woman with a limp, she had a great walk, enhanced by the snug fit of her trousers and the way her blouse nipped in at the waist.

"Where is my niece?" he asked as he took off his leather jacket and hooked it on the back of a chair at the side of her desk. Sitting down, he crossed Levi's-clad legs, and perched his rain-speckled hat on his knee.

"I sent her to the library with an aide." She scooped up a few plastic shapes and scattered them in front of Colin. The baby squealed in delight as he pounded his hands and scattered them.

"You're sure good with kids," he said.

"It's a plus in my occupation."

"Do you have any of your own?"

She seemed to flinch at his question, but answered quickly enough. "No, but my brother and his wife have seven-month-old quadruplet girls. I'm very close to them."

"Local?" he asked, thinking of that flinch. After ten years in the Bureau, he'd learned to read people pretty well and to trust his instincts. Those instincts now said there were nuances here that aroused his curiosity. Ms. Bishop might look put together on the outside, but inside, he'd be willing to bet, there were troubles.

He instantly chided himself. He wasn't an agent anymore and she wasn't a desperado. What had driven him to invade her personal space by asking about children? He made a mental note to knock it off.

"No, my family lives up closer to Seattle, in a little town called Westerly."

"I imagine you're planning to go home for the holidays," he said, unsure why he kept questioning her, just intrigued by the undercurrents.

She blinked a time or two and said, "No, not this year," and in what appeared to be a blatant attempt to get the discussion back to him, added, "I want to be honest with you. Even though I've only been in Shay a couple of weeks, I've heard quite a bit about you."

"Uh-oh."

"Don't look so nervous."

"Where did you hear about me?"

"Here and there. The teachers' lounge."

"Gossip," he said.

She shrugged. "I wouldn't call it that. Concern for Noelle, intrigue over you—"

"Me?"

She titled her head. "You're a hometown boy who left the family ranch and joined the FBI. Plus you're a bona fide hero."

"That hero stuff is way overblown," he said, repositioning his hat, hoping she'd let it drop.

"Modesty aside, you saved everybody on an overturned bus right here in your own hometown. That's heroic."

"Not everyone," he said, glancing away from her blue eyes and down at Colin. The baby had abandoned the blocks and now lay sprawled against Faith's breasts, fingers curled in her ruffled blouse, eyes drooping, perfectly content. What male wouldn't be in such a position?

"I didn't know," she said gently. "I was under the impression everyone got out."

"There was an older woman trapped under a seat—" He stopped talking again as his nostrils seemed to fill with the smell of gasoline, his head with the screams of the trapped woman. He shifted in his chair.

"I'm sorry I've made you uncomfortable," she said. "I didn't realize…"

The truth was, he was used to being the one who knew things about other people, and he was finding he didn't much like being on the other end of things. "It's okay. People talk."

"But not unkindly. You shouldn't think that."

"Well, it's water under the bridge," he said. "Old news."

His next thought made his blood run cold. *Was it old news? It had happened less than five months ago when he came home to see his dying mother. There'd been a newspaper article, too, despite the Bureau's attempt to keep it hush-hush.*

What about Neil Roberts? All the escaped man had to do was hit a library computer and do a little digging.

Trip's jaw tightened. He had to get back to the

ranch, alert people, get a picture of Roberts and pass it around. But not now. For fifteen more minutes he was here to focus on Noelle, not Neil Roberts.

At first he was relieved when she brought the subject of the meeting back in focus. "Noelle is a great kid," she said.

"Yeah—"

"A little shy, but you know that."

"She's been through a lot," he said, narrowing his eyes.

"I know."

"But she's resilient. She'll be okay."

"I'm sure she will. I know she will."

"Losing her folks was hard on her," he said gruffly.

"And on you, too, Mr. Tripper. Hard on all of you."

Here it came, the "How To Help Noelle" speech. Hell, maybe she had an idea or two on how to fix him, too. Very carefully, he said, "I think Noelle is coping as well as can be expected. She needs stability and time—"

"Mr. Tripper? Please don't get the idea I have anything negative to say about Noelle, or your parenting, either, for that matter."

A big knot Trip hadn't even been aware of seemed to unravel in his gut. "I guess I'm getting defensive," he admitted slowly. "I'm new at this."

"Noelle and Colin are lucky kids to have you. Not all uncles would be willing to change their lives and step in when needed."

He nodded, feeling uneasy with accolades he knew he didn't deserve. He'd done what needed to be done, sure, but he'd had to give himself a few stern lectures along the way. At thirty-seven years of age, it was no easy trick going from self-centered bachelor agent to single dad in the course of a day or two.

He glanced back at Faith in time to witness her smothering a yawn with her hand. She'd done it a couple of times already, and up close, bluish smudges showed under her eyes. When she caught him watching her, she shook her head. "I'm so sorry."

"Keeping late hours?"

"Not intentionally."

"Excuse me?" he asked, intrigued.

She took a deep breath, seemingly on the edge of explaining, and then she shied away, glancing down at Colin again, running fingers lightly over his spiky hair.

Undercurrents. Issues. He'd bet the ranch she was in trouble, but what kind he couldn't imagine. She didn't seem the kind for trouble with the law— that left family, and she'd said she had no family here. That didn't mean there wasn't a boyfriend, however. So, what was worrying her at home? Something to do with the scars on her face and the limp?

"This isn't fair," he said.

"What isn't?"

"You know all about me and I know nothing about you."

"There's not much to know," she said.

"Married?"

"No."

"Attached?"

"Mr. Tripper, really. The details of my life aren't pertinent."

"And yet, you aren't getting enough sleep," he said with a smile, to let her know he was on her side.

"It's not like I'm teaching Driver's Ed," she said.

He laughed at that. "Okay, Ms. Bishop, I'll mind my own business."

Her smile held a note of wistfulness, almost as though she wished he'd push her harder. Mixed signals from this woman, that was for sure. Signals he wouldn't mind getting to understand. Call it professional curiosity.

Sure.

She added, "Please, call me Faith."

"Faith," he repeated. It was a good name for her. "I'm Luke Tripper, but everyone calls me Trip. Now, tell me more about Noelle."

She opened a folder with Noelle's name on it and started handing him papers. He examined all the drawings and the handwriting samples of the child's ABCs and listened to how bright Noelle was and how they wanted to test her and maybe put her in an accelerated program. During all this, he wondered what his sister would have done, what she would have wanted. This kind of thought played in his head on a daily basis, as he transitioned from glorified nanny to daddy. He was it. He was all these kids had. The only question was—would he be enough?

He came back into the moment when she dropped her voice. Colin had fallen asleep and she held him close, as though by second nature.

"My own mother died when I was about six, so I can identify with Noelle," she said. "I don't know what I would have done without my dad and my big brother, Zac. Anyway, I know pretty well what Noelle is going through." She met his eyes. "So, if there's anything I can do to make it easier for her, I would love to help. In or out of school, whenever. This is the first time I've lived outside of Westerly, away from my family, you know, so I have plenty of free time…." Her voice petered out and she shook her head again. "Listen to me go on and on."

"It's a very kind offer," he said—and meant it. "Right now, though—"

He stopped when his cell phone rang. He had it out of his pocket and had checked the ID number before he realized he should have just let it ring. Years of always being on call had formed habits he was finding hard to break. Smiling apologetically at Faith, he said, "It's my house. I think I'd better take it. I'm sorry—"

"Go ahead," she urged.

"Trip here," he said, and listened as Mrs. Murphy, his housekeeper, identified herself.

"Everything okay? This isn't a good time—"

"No, everything's not okay, and that's a fact. Here I am at the house alone and you off with the wee ones," the older woman said and proceeded to elaborate, her Irish brogue growing more pronounced the more agitated she became. He felt his own blood pressure rise as she spoke. A minute or two later, he clicked off the phone with the assurance he would take care of things.

Faith was staring at him, and the serious set of her very attractive mouth announced his own tension hadn't been lost on her. "What's wrong?" she whispered.

"I'm not sure."

Her fingers brushed her scarred cheek and disappeared into her hair as she said, "I don't mean to pry, it's just that you look so concerned."

"You're not prying, Faith. That was my housekeeper. She got home from her dentist appointment to find the police out at the ranch. They told her they discovered our babysitter's car abandoned by a minimart, with the keys in the ignition."

"That sounds odd, doesn't it?"

"Yes and no. Gina's car is one busted fan belt away from the junkyard. She often parks on inclines, in case the engine won't start. She says she hopes someone will steal it so she can collect the insurance."

"Which doesn't explain why you look the way you do."

"No," he said. It was one thing to leave your keys in the ignition out at the ranch, another on a city street. Face it, his gut was telling him something was wrong and obviously the police felt the same way.

How long would it take Neil Roberts to get to Shay, Washington? Less than a day. He'd had the time, maybe, though not knowing more of the details made assessing things like time difficult. But even if Roberts had gotten here, how or why would he connect Gina Cooke with Luke Tripper?

"I have to go," he said, getting to his feet. "I need to talk to the police." He pulled his hat on his head, grabbed his jacket, then looked down at the still-seated Faith, who had both arms wrapped around his slumbering nephew. Pausing, he took a deep breath. "Damn, I actually forgot about the kids for a moment."

"Leave them with me," she said, picking up a pen and quickly scribbling a number on a paper. "This is my cell. Call me when you get done doing whatever you have to do. I'll take care of Noelle and Colin."

"I couldn't ask you to do that."

"You didn't ask me."

"I'll call Mrs. Murphy to come get them."

"In this weather? Just leave Colin's car seat in the front office."

"You don't know what you're in for with that car seat," he warned her. He dug a card out of his wallet and handed it to her. "The second number reaches my cell phone. Call me if you need me. Meanwhile, tell me where you live and I'll come get them in, say, an hour?"

"Well, actually, I have a few things I need to do. Just call my cell and we'll meet. The kids won't be in the way, don't worry."

Something was odd here, but he had the overriding feeling time was of the essence for Gina, so he let it go. "Thank you." Before he left the room, he turned. Faith had gotten to her feet, the slumbering baby draped across her shoulder. She stood silhouetted against the gray skies visible through the windows at her back, her golden hair reflecting the indoor light. She looked at him expectantly, and all he could do was stare.

He had the oddest feeling about her.

"Is there something else?" she asked.

He shook his head and left.

Chapter Two

Half an hour later, Faith found out what she was getting into with Colin's car seat. The sedan seemed to reverberate with the baby's outraged protest.

"Noelle, honey, could you give Colin a toy or a cracker or something?" Faith asked, voice raised to be heard.

Noelle, strapped into the back next to her brother, said, "It won't work, Ms. Bishop. Nothing works in the car."

"I thought babies liked to go for rides," Faith said, thinking of her nieces who always seemed to quiet down once the engine started.

"Not Colin," Noelle yelled with what sounded like a hint of pride.

The weather hadn't changed, except that the skies were darker than ever. Faith tried to think of somewhere besides her apartment where she could take small children and could think of nothing. Shay didn't have a mall or an indoor playground, and she hadn't had a chance to make any friends outside the school.

"Where are we going?" Noelle asked, her voice smaller now, unsure, barely audible over her brother's tirade.

"I don't know," Faith mumbled. And then, because there really wasn't another choice, she added, "My place."

After a few moments, Colin's cries grew a little less raucous, and as Faith negotiated the wet streets, she thought back to her meeting with Luke Tripper.

As she'd confessed to him, she'd heard about him first from the teacher she replaced, and then around the school. The bus story had intrigued her from the moment she heard it, maybe because she'd brushed against evil last spring, barely surviving a malicious attack. To hear about a man who ran back and forth to an overturned bus risking his life to save others reassured her in some odd way that people were still good. The look in his eyes when he admitted he hadn't saved everyone had touched her deeply.

So she'd wondered what he would be like—and had built a mental image of a hero: strong, fearless, able to leap tall buildings. Luke Tripper looked as though he was all those things.

He was as tall as her brother, Zac, but not as

lanky, more muscular, broad-shouldered, body trim and fit, thick, dark hair cut short. And those eyes. Smoldering, yes, but also focused and intense. She'd found herself struggling not to tell him her deepest, darkest secrets.

Add to that a sophisticated air at odds with boots and jeans and a hat that looked as though it had been around the block a time or two. That inconsistency was due, no doubt, to the fact he'd only been a rancher for four or five months. Before that he'd been an FBI agent, rumored to have done covert work. The veneer left over from that career no doubt explained her desire to confide in him. Only her pledge to herself that she would solve her own problems kept her mouth shut.

Besides, Trip had enough troubles of his own.

Faith fought against a stab of pure, unadulterated self-pity. Sure, she missed Puget Sound, old friends and family, but she was in debt up to her eyeballs with medical bills and Shay was the only place she could find a decent job.

There was another reason for her decision to move, too, and it had to do with her father and brother. Last May, Zac had married Olivia, Faith's best friend, and had adopted her four little girls. He was sheriff in Westerly, his life was busy and full, and he was happier than Faith had ever seen him. Meanwhile, after twenty years of being a widower, her father had discovered love right in his own backyard with Olivia's mother, Juliet Hart. The two were getting married in Hawaii over the holidays. Faith had told them she was too busy with her new job to travel to explain why she wouldn't be at the ceremony. She hadn't wanted to admit the truth: she couldn't afford the trip. She hadn't confided in either her father or her brother that her insurance hadn't begun to cover expenses.

The point was, both the men in her life had moved on, and yet she knew their happiness was affected by her own sense of detachment, and it killed her. She was tired of pretending everything was okay and was determined to solve her own problems.

Where did that leave the little ache in her gut when she thought about Luke Tripper? In her gut, she supposed, buried and secret where it belonged.

Faith's apartment was actually the basement of a two-story house in the worst corner of the worst part of Shay. The price for paying off her mountainous medical bills was living in a terrible neighborhood with a landlady named Ruby Lee who gave Faith the heebie-jeebies.

As she drove around the house to reach her private entrance in the back, some of her tension dissipated. The main garage was closed and the house looked dark. Hallelujah, it appeared Ruby wasn't home. Faith parked under the lean-to attached to the garage.

"This is where you live?" Noelle asked as Faith helped her unbuckle her seat belt and collect her backpack. Noelle looked a lot like her uncle. Same dark brown hair, only on Noelle it was long and braided. Same deep brown eyes.

Faith took Colin out of his seat. The baby grabbed her around the neck and immediately stopped fussing, rubbing his damp eyes with a plump fist. Poor little guy looked tired.

"This is where I live," Faith said as the rain pounded the fiberglass roof of the lean-to. Holding tightly to Colin and the diaper bag Trip had left in the school office, she took Noelle's hand. "Let's run between the raindrops to the front porch, okay?"

They dashed the ten feet to the feeble overhang covering the door. Faith struggled to keep up with Noelle, her left leg protesting a bit at the unevenness of the ground.

Juggling baby and belongings, Faith dug for her keys. She found they were unnecessary, as the door pushed open when she touched the knob. Had she forgotten to lock up when she left that morning?

No way. She couldn't take the children into a compromised house. For a second she stood there, unsure what to do.

As she raced through her options, the porch light went on and the door opened wide.

Faith gasped as Noelle shrank back against her legs. A man of about twenty stood facing them. Dressed in black denim jeans and a torn black sweatshirt with a metallic lightning bolt bisecting the front, muscles bulged in his arms, jet black hair flopped over his forehead. He held a hammer in one hand.

"David," Faith said, catching her breath and laying her free hand on Noelle's damp shoulder. "You scared me."

"I came to fix the cabinet you told Ma was bothering you." His gaze slid to Faith's hips and stayed there.

"Did your mother let you into my place?"

"I have my own key."

"Your own key? Who gave you a key?" she demanded.

"I'm helping Ma. I'm taking care of things around here from now on. I'm taking care of you."

Like hell you are, Faith thought. "Are you finished with the cabinet?"

"Almost." He turned and walked back into the heavily shadowed room, disappearing into the kitchen alcove.

"Let's get out of the rain," Faith said, shepherding Noelle inside, turning on lights, trying to dispel some of the gloom. The basement, which she'd rented furnished, looked even worse with bright lights. There wasn't a single Christmas decoration, and Faith could only imagine how cheerless it struck a five-year-old. The child stayed right against her legs as a few banging noises came from the kitchen.

"It's done," David said, appearing in the opening between Faith's very modest living room and the kitchen. "You want to check it?"

"No. I'm sure it's fine."

David looked at Noelle again, then at Colin. "Ma said no kids."

"I'm just watching them—they don't live here."

"Oh."

"Well, thanks. But next time, please make an appointment."

He lifted one lip, revealing a pointed incisor.

The door opened behind Faith. She and both children swiveled to look at the newcomer. Ruby Lee bustled into the room, closing the door behind her, sandwiching Faith, Colin and Noelle between herself and her son. She wore a black rain coat and silver rain boots, a silver rain hat riddled with holes, tied under her chin. Her makeup looked as though it been applied with a trowel. If today ran true to form, within six hours she'd be drunk, pounding on Faith's door, makeup sliding down her cheeks.

"You fix the cabinet?" Ruby asked.

David's reply sounded sullen. "Yeah."

"Then go check the bathroom door."

"Oh, that's okay," Faith said quickly.

"You told me it wouldn't lock," Ruby said, narrowing her eyes.

"It doesn't, but right now I have guests—"

"Now or never," David said, stepping closer to Faith, his overmuscled body radiating a primal heat that made Faith want to gasp for air. She retreated toward Ruby. He added, "No time like the present, right?"

"I said no kids," Ruby said, staring at Colin. For the first time, Faith realized Colin's tiny fingers had clutched her coat collar so tight it strained against her throat, half choking her. Could the baby sense the tension?

"Will you please both leave?" Faith asked.

"There's work to be done. David is here now," Ruby insisted, her eyes slightly unfocused, as though she'd started drinking early today.

"Then we'll leave," Faith said.

"You don't gotta go," David said, lifting the hammer, flexing his muscles. "Come show me what you want done. Ma can watch the babies while I…service you."

"I'm not watching no kids," Ruby said.

Faith's mouth had gone dry at the innuendo in David's voice. She looked at Ruby again, hoping her landlady would intercede; but that was dumb, help wasn't coming from that quarter. She repeated, "If you won't go, we will. But before we do, let me make myself clear. I don't like people having keys to my home, not even you, David. It undermines my feeling of safety."

"This ain't your place, it's mine," Ruby reminded her. "And what's mine is David's."

David advanced again, his gaze challenging. "Maybe you want me to come back later tonight after you dump the kids. Maybe you want a little one-on-one."

It was all Faith could do not to punch him. She gritted her teeth and said, "Absolutely not."

He narrowed his eyes. "You too good for me, is that it, *Miss* Bishop?"

At that particular moment, Faith didn't know what to do about this situation, but she did know she wasn't going to subject either child to another moment of it. Without answering David, she reached around Ruby and opened the front door. Noelle practically bolted, running back to the car heedless of the rain or the puddles.

Even Colin's enraged screams as Faith backed down the driveway were a better alternative than one more moment in that basement hellhole. She glanced back once to see David standing in her open door, holding the hammer in one hand, tapping it into the open palm of the other, his belligerent gaze tracking her retreat.

THIS WAS THE FIRST TIME since Trip had returned to Shay that he'd had cause to go to the police station. The accident he'd been involved with earlier in the year had been handled by the highway patrol, while the fire that claimed the life of his sister and her husband had been investigated by the sheriff's department, since the ranch wasn't within the Shay city limits.

He'd heard rumors the department wasn't run very well and, as he stepped up to the counter and found himself eye-to-eye with a kid wearing a slipshod uniform and reading a comic book, his expectations fell even further.

"I want to talk to whoever is in charge of the Gina Cooke investigation," Trip said.

The kid looked blank. "Gina who?"

"Is there a detective here, maybe? Your boss?"

Now the boy looked more comfortable. "You want to talk to the Chief?"

"Sure."

The boy nodded, turned around and hollered, "Chief Novak? Someone here to see you."

"Thomas Novak?"

"Yeah. You know him?"

At that moment, a ticked-off-looking man about

Trip's age strode into the front area from the back. He wore a tight green uniform, buttons straining down the front. Heavy black frames perched ponderously on the bridge of his nose. Glaring at the teenager, he said, "Damn it, Lenny, how many times have I told you come get me, don't shout?" He looked up from the cowering Lenny, met Trip's eyes and rocked back on his heels. "I'll be."

"It's been a long time," Trip said. "You're 'Chief'?"

"That's right. I heard you were back out at the ranch. Sorry about your sister and her husband. Hell of a thing."

"Thank you," Trip said. If Lenny hadn't called Novak by name, Trip was pretty sure he would never have merged the skinny kid from their high school days with the corpulent man standing in front of him. "We need to talk."

"You here about Gina Cooke?"

"That's right. I have some information you might want—"

"See that, Lenny," Novak interrupted, as he took off his glasses and began polishing the lenses with a tissue he plucked from a box on the counter. "Mr. Tripper here is a FBI big shot but he's going to take the time to help us out. Isn't that nice?"

Lenny slid Trip a glance.

"Gina is my babysitter," Trip said. "And I'm no longer with the Bureau."

"I know that."

"You went out to my place when you found her car—"

"I was just following procedures. The hunt is over."

"You found here? Where?"

"We haven't found her, but we figured out what happened. She ran off with that boyfriend of hers."

"Peter Saks?"

"Yeah."

"My housekeeper said you found Gina's car abandoned."

Novak folded his glasses into his shirt pocket and leaned on the counter, resting his weight on his forearms. "Her car was found outside the Quik Mart on Apple Street. She apparently stopped there every day to buy a cup of coffee before heading out to your place. What got a pedestrian to call in was she'd left the window open and the rain was pouring in. Then there were the keys in the ignition."

"A bad habit of hers," Trip said.

"That's what I hear. We sent someone out to your place to see if she showed up for work and someone else to talk to the girl's boyfriend and her mother. The mother said Gina always leaves her keys in the ignition and that she and the boyfriend had a fight. The boyfriend wasn't at home, neighbors said he packed up this morning and told them he was going on vacation." He shrugged. "That Quik Mart is right on the way to the interstate. We figure Saks ran across her, maybe even waited for her to show up there if he knew it was her habit to stop. Maybe he talked her into a little make-up trip. It looks like she decided to go with him. End of story."

Novak straightened and looked at Trip as though daring him to challenge these conclusions.

"And Gina's mother is comfortable with this supposition?" Trip asked after a long moment of debating whether to share his suspicions about Neil Roberts with the chief.

"Says it makes perfect sense. Says her daughter was a pushover for Peter Saks."

"Where did Saks go, exactly?"

"The neighbors don't know. Camping, maybe."

"In this weather? In December?"

"Maybe he went south. Hell, it's a free country."

Trip stared at Novak. "I can see where you're coming from, but the fact Gina didn't call bothers me. It's not like her to just leave."

"There you're wrong," Novak said. "Her mother said she ran off without a word a year or two ago."

Trip hadn't known that. "Gina told me Saks had a history of domestic violence."

Chief Novak flipped his hand. "The boy's a hothead, that's all." The big man heaved a sigh that put even greater pressure on his buttons and added, "Listen. I know you had a fancy career in the FBI. I bet it sucks to be out of the action. But this is *my* town, so why don't you just go back to ranching?" Novak slapped his hands on the counter. Case closed.

Trip left before his temper got the better of him.

IT WAS GETTING DARK. The rain had let up, but the temperature had dropped, making the roads icy. Faith had taken the children to a big-box store where she changed Colin's diaper and fed him some of the dry cereal and fruit she found in the diaper bag. She'd bought Noelle a banana, they'd returned to her car and now it seemed the baby had fallen asleep. By the hush in the backseat, Faith thought it likely Noelle had nodded off as well.

How had her life gotten to this point?

Six months before, she'd known who she was and what she wanted. It had been her friend, Olivia, who wanted out of Westerly, not Faith. And now she was driving two very small children around on a stormy night in a town she barely knew, while their uncle tried to find their babysitter. To add insult to injury, she couldn't even take them somewhere decent, somewhere warm, somewhere safe because her landlady and her son made the Bates Hotel seem like a day spa.

"Ms. Bishop?" Noelle said. Guess she wasn't asleep after all.

"Yes, sweetie?"

"Can we go home?"

Home. "Well, I don't want to run into those people again—"

"*My* home," Noelle said. "Mrs. Murphy makes cookies sometimes."

They were at the northeast edge of town. Faith knew Trip lived on a ranch with the children, she knew about where it was, as she'd passed a sign on one of her weekend drives. It was called the Triple T.

Dare she drive to his house? Would he think she was being pushy? Did it matter what he thought?

"What kind of cookies?" she asked as she headed out to the highway. At this point, any decision was better than no decision.

"Sometimes chocolate with peanuts, only Uncle Trip doesn't like peanuts, so now she leaves them out."

"I sure hope she made some today," Faith said.

"Me, too." It was quiet for a mile or two, and

then Noelle spoke again, her voice ominous this time. "Uh-oh, Ms. Bishop."

"What's wrong?"

"Colin is waking up."

IT WAS ALMOST DARK by the time Trip pulled up in front of the Quik Mart. Gina's car was nowhere in sight. For a second, it crossed his mind she'd come back for it, or her mother had taken it or the cops had impounded it, and then he remembered the way Gina always parked on a hillside, facing down, when she came to the ranch, in case the engine wouldn't start. There was a slope beyond the store. He topped the hill and looked down the road that bordered a ravine on one side and a few stores on the other side, and sure enough, there was Gina's car, pointed downhill.

Gina's car windows were up now and the doors were locked. The car itself looked like it always did, battered and old, the tattered front seat bare, except for a fluff of something very white and purple, just visible on the passenger side, stuffed between seat and seat back. Trip hitched his hands on his waist and looked up and down the street. A gas station on the corner, a flower shop and a shoe repair directly opposite. He checked his watch and decided he could spare a few more minutes.

The man in the shoe repair shop worked in the

back and came to the front only when he heard the
bell ring over the door. Trip asked him about the
car across the street, but the repairman hadn't even
noticed the police, let alone a nineteen-year-old
woman. He did say he'd seen the car there before.

The flower shop was better staffed. The three
female employees, all in their thirties and all
smiling up a storm, agreed they'd seen Gina's car
parked on the hillside before, but none of them had
actually seen her, not today, anyway. Since Trip
didn't have a photo to show around, there wasn't
much else to be learned.

He went to the service station last. It was an in-
dependently owned station, with higher prices than
could be found elsewhere, hence it appeared to do
a neighborhood kind of business. There were no
cars at the pumps, but there was a man in the
garage, sitting on an overturned box, lights blazing
around him. It looked as though he was in the
process of dismantling an engine.

Trip stood there for a moment, watching. Late
twenties, pudgy, somehow familiar, dressed in blue
coveralls, extremely focused on his job. The
mechanic was picking up little pieces and wiping
them with a grease rag, dropping some into some
kind of solvent, arranging others in a pattern of sorts.

The guy gave no indication he was aware of
Trip. Mindful of the need for haste, Trip stepped
into the light and said, "Sorry to bother you…"

At the sound of Trip's voice, the attendant jumped up. Sandy hair, sparse mustache over full lips, blue eyes, a couple of grease smudges on his cheek. His overalls were too big for him. "Sorry, sir, I didn't hear you drive in."

"I didn't drive in, I walked. I don't need gas, I just want to ask you a couple of questions." As the mechanic perched back atop his box, Trip added, "You look like you know what you're doing with that engine."

"Been taking 'em apart since I was a little kid."

"You look familiar," Trip said. "You from around here?" Too late he realized he'd fallen into interrogation mode.

The kid didn't seem to mind. "More or less," he said.

Trip introduced himself and stepped closer, hand extended.

"Eddie Reed," the guy replied, but raised grease-stained hands to explain why he didn't return the shake. He added, "I know who you are, Mr. Tripper. I came to your place looking for work a few weeks ago."

"I don't—"

"Your foreman, that Mr. Plum guy, he said you just hired someone else."

A big clock on the wall ticked away another ten seconds before Trip added, "I'm wondering about the car across the street. The green one that's been parked there most of today."

"What about it?"

"Did you see the young woman who left it there this morning?"

"I don't come to work till two o'clock," Eddie said. "What does she look like?"

"Oh, around twenty, long red hair, tall. Pretty girl."

"She special to you?"

Trip ignored the question. "Did you see anyone matching her description?"

"No, sorry. I saw the cops nosing around, that's all. Is something wrong?"

"I'm not sure. Probably not."

This earned Trip a long glance, until Eddie, apparently losing interest, went back to his task with a nimble-fingered finesse Trip envied. How did a man get that comfortable with engines? At his father's knee? Trip thought of his own father, the man who had started the Triple T Ranch, the man who could fix anything, the man Trip had given up emulating two decades before.

"Thanks anyway," Trip said.

"Sure. Hey, I hope it works out."

"You hope what works out?"

"The girl. I hope you find her."

"Yeah," Trip said. "Thanks."

Walking out of the garage, Trip dug from his

pocket the paper on which Faith had written her number. Standing in the light shining through the gas station window, he flipped open his cell phone right as it rang.

"Trip here."

"This is Faith—"

"I was just going to call you."

"Listen to me," she pleaded. Her voice sounded anxious and in the background, he heard Colin screaming.

"What—"

"I'm on the road to your house with your kids. Someone is following really close behind me, so close his lights blind me and I've tried to get away from him, but he speeds up when I do."

"Where are you exactly?" he yelled as he ran to his truck. None of this made any sense. Why was she driving the kids out to the ranch?

"I don't know where I am, not exactly, but there are hardly any cars out here. I passed something called Tyrone Gardens a few minutes ago."

"I'm coming," he said, estimating time in his head. "Don't stop, whatever you do, and don't speed up if you can help it. I'll call ahead to the ranch. I know where you are... I'll be there."

"Okay," she said, almost drowned out by a high-pitched scream that had to be Noelle. His gut tightened as she whispered, "Oh, please hurry."

Chapter Three

Noelle screamed again, "It's closer!"

"Noelle, sit down! Make sure your seat belt is tight."

Colin suddenly grew very quiet. While it was a tremendous relief, it was also a concern. Faith dare not turn to make sure the child was okay. "Check Colin, Noelle. Is he all right?"

"I—I think he's scared," Noelle managed.

"Hold his hand, okay?"

"Okay," Noelle said, and Faith could hear the tears in her voice.

In the next instant, the lights inside grew even brighter, Faith's car seemed to pause and the abandoned road seemed to hum.

A premonition gripped Faith. He was going to ram her. She knew it. "Noelle, hang on—"

The words had barely left her lips when the impact came. Her car lurched forward, the tires spinning as she hit the verge on the side of the road. Trying to drown out the unsettling sounds of the children shrieking, Faith fought the wheel as the tires drifted over icy weeds until they ran up against a berm, sending the car bouncing back toward the road. The truck had dropped back a few feet, but Faith knew what would happen next, she knew it would advance again.

"Talk to me, Noelle. Are you and Colin still okay?"

"I think so," Noelle sputtered.

"Keep your head down, sing to Colin, we're almost home."

The cat-and-mouse game had started after she turned off the main highway. According to the sign, she had five miles to endure before they reached the ranch. Time was passing in a frenzy. She wasn't even sure how long ago she'd called Trip, just that she'd tossed her purse back to Noelle and directed the little girl to find the flashlight and her uncle's card buried in the front pocket.

Considering how afraid Noelle had to be, Faith thought it pretty amazing she could so calmly read the right set of numbers to her, so she could punch them into the phone. Now the tiny beam of the pocket flashlight flickered on and off as Noelle apparently used it to check on Colin.

But even if Trip showed up right now, what could he do…how could he stop this?

Who was back there? It had to be a madman, and the only madman she knew was David Lee. Had he followed her, had he waited while she and the kids went into the store, then tracked her again, hanging back in traffic and biding his time until she turned onto a desolate stretch of highway?

Why would he do something like this? She was almost positive the pursuing vehicle was a truck, as the headlights were higher off the ground than her own. Did David drive a truck? She didn't know. She'd never actually seen him come and go from his mother's place. He must park on the street.

The lights were once again coming closer. She instinctively pressed down on the accelerator pedal. She heard Trip's voice warning her not to speed up, but the thought of being bumped again terrified her. The lights swerved off to the lane beside her and for one glorious moment, she thought her pursuer was giving up, that maybe he was getting ahead of her so he could speed away.

She could see now: it was a truck, a dark truck, though she couldn't see the driver. It pulled up parallel to her and she eased up on the gas, falling back, willing him to keep on going. It looked like it was working, when suddenly the truck swerved into her car, hitting the front bumper.

She held on to the wheel and yelled at the children to cover their heads, or at least that was her intention, but words were lost in the screams that bounced around the interior of the car. Her vehicle flew off the road and straight up a steep bank until it breasted the top and became airborne. It landed a second later with a crash, spinning until it came to a clattering halt.

TRIP TURNED HIS LIGHTS on high beam. As he raced out of town, he'd called the ranch foreman, George Plum, and the two men had agreed to drive toward one another until they either found Faith and her pursuer or met on the road.

Trip saw the approaching headlights a half-mile away. As it was a straight stretch of highway, he could see there was no one behind him, so he slowed down. George Plum pulled his ranch truck up beside him and the two men rolled down their windows.

"Anything?" Trip said, his breath condensing.

George shook his graying head. The seriousness of the situation was manifested by the fact that George, for once, wasn't puffing on a pipe. "You didn't see nothing, either?"

"No. She described a chase of some kind, but it's obviously over. Did you run across anyone else between here and the ranch?"

George shook his head. "Not a thing. But if you know the area, there are any number of little roads to use to get back to Highway 67 before you get to the ranch."

"Yeah. Okay, I'll head to the ranch, keeping an eye out in case he ran her off the road. You go toward the Tyrone Gardens exit. We'll meet back at the Triple T."

"You got it," George said, and rolling up his window, he drove off.

Trip flipped his headlights back to high beam and started searching the side of the road up ahead as he drove slowly along the highway. He found a spot with what looked like fresh tire marks on the grassy edge and got out to check it with a flashlight. Nothing there, so he got back in the truck, fighting a sinking feeling that wouldn't go away.

The tracks were new. How new he couldn't tell, but new enough it was possible they were made by Faith's car, and they brought home the reality of her situation. The icy night, the slick road, the frightened children, the panic.

What was going on? Could this be the work of Neil Roberts? The timing seemed too tight to finger Roberts. The man was brighter than your average serial killer, but he wasn't psychic. So how could he have connected Faith to Trip, unless he'd been trailing Trip, seen Trip depart the school alone, then stayed around to see Faith leave with the children. How had he put it all together?

It seemed a long shot. But, oh, God, if that man got his hands on the kids or Faith…

He found another spot in the frozen mud, with deep tracks that looked pretty fresh. His gut told him this was it. He took a moment to unlock the shotgun from the back window and load it. He labored up an incline, slipping and sliding with each step. The ground was torn, mud oozing like dark blood from a fresh wound. Upon reaching the top, he shined his flashlight in an arc and found himself staring at a gray sedan about thirty yards away. The passenger side of the car was pressed up against three or four pines and a pile of rocks.

He slid down the incline and ran across the ground to the car, reaching it before he'd so much as taken a breath, his heartbeat thundering in his head. If Noelle had been on the passenger side in the backseat she'd be crushed against the trees.

The sharp sound of a baby crying reached his ears as he yanked on the front door. Locked. He yelled and banged, his usual calm in a crisis fleeing in the face of the fact that these children were his responsibility—

He shined the light in the window. Faith Bishop, Noelle and Colin all looked back at him, eyes wide, mouths open, their combined screams penetrating the glass. And then a tiny beam of light hit him on the face. The front door lock popped open and they tumbled out all at once, as though glued together. With tears running down each of their faces, they all looked as though they'd faced a firing squad and the guns had misfired.

He gathered them into his arms, crushing Colin against his chest, his gun arm wrapped around Faith's back, Noelle pressed against his legs.

"Are you okay? Are you all okay?" he asked, straining to shine the flashlight, looking for cuts and bruises.

"We're just so glad to see you," Faith gasped. "I didn't know if I should chance taking them out of the car. My tank was almost empty and I didn't smell gasoline, but—"

"You did fine," he interrupted. "You're all okay, it's a miracle."

"I think my cell phone hit Colin in the forehead and Noelle says her arm hurts."

He leaned down and shone the light in Noelle's eyes. She blinked and turned away. As he stood back up and reached for Colin, the little girl flung herself at Faith who lifted her from the ground and hugged her. The beam from the tiny flashlight still clutched in Noelle's hand pointed heavenward as their breath misted around their heads.

Colin's bump looked superficial in the wavering light of the flashlight, and there was nothing weak about his grip on Trip's jacket. The baby nuzzled

Trip's neck, his nose like a little ice cube against Trip's warmer skin.

"Retrieve what you need from your car," he told Faith as she set Noelle on the ground. "Let's get out of here."

"Before he comes back," Faith said, her voice trembling.

"He's not coming back, not tonight."

"But—"

"Trust me," Trip said, jaw tightening.

No, a coward like this man would not return to finish the job, especially not when he saw Trip's truck. Whoever did this had to know he'd run his victim's car off the road. If he'd been intent on murder, he would have come after it, not driven away.

And that didn't sound like Neil Roberts.

FAITH SHARED THE FRONT SEAT with both children. Colin was very quiet, his body heavy and limp. Noelle's head drooped against Faith's arm.

Faith, on the other hand, was so wired she almost shook. She strained against her seat belt to peer ahead into the night and glance in the rearview mirror attached to the passenger door, ready to jump out of her skin if she caught sight of approaching lights from either direction.

Beside her, Trip called someone named George

and told him everyone was safe, to come back to the ranch. Safe? She didn't feel safe, not even enclosed in the big, warm truck, not even with Trip less than a foot away. She doubted she'd ever feel safe again.

She was so wound up in the lingering effects of the terrifying last hour or so that she jumped as the truck rattled over a cattle guard and under a huge wooden arc announcing the Triple T Ranch. Looking out into the dark fields, she said, "Where are all the cows?"

"Most are down in the winter pastures," Trip replied.

As he spoke the headlights illuminated a pair of giant fir trees looming like sentinels on either side of the road. Trip drove past them into a large paved area flanked by a sprawling ranch-style house ablaze with lights. An equally well-lit barn and the dark shapes of a half-dozen other buildings loomed in the distance.

Trip hadn't yet shut down the engine when the door of the house sprang open and a handful of people rushed outside.

"I take it they know about the car chase," Faith said.

"Looks like it," Trip said as a heavyset woman with graying red hair opened the passenger door. Bypassing Faith, she crooned assurances to Colin in a lilting Irish brogue as she lifted him from Faith's arms. An older man asked Noelle if she was all right as he liberated her from the seat belt. Holding the children in protective embraces, they moved off with the others, voices raised as they re-entered the house, leaving Trip and Faith alone in the sudden hush.

Trip slammed the truck door and came around to her side. "You're awfully quiet, Faith. Are you sure you're not hurt?"

"Just shaky," she said.

His fingers were warm and strong as they grasped her hand and gently pulled her from the truck. She landed in front of him. She found his closeness both reassuring and frightening; that much raw male energy was unsettling, but in a totally different way than David Lee's proximity.

"Thank you," he said as he released her hand.

Blinking her eyes, she looked up him. "Thank you for what? For almost getting your niece and nephew killed?"

"No, for keeping your head and driving so well no one was seriously injured. In my book, that deserves a thank you."

"If I hadn't exposed them to David Lee, they wouldn't have been in danger in the first place."

He grew very still, intimidating in his utter silence, until he finally said, "Who the hell is David Lee?"

"My landlady's son."

"He's the one who did this? You saw his face or recognized his vehicle?"

"No, I didn't see anyone's face, and the vehicle was just a dark truck, maybe even a van. But it must have been David. Who else would it be?"

Trip shook his head, and though she couldn't see his expression clearly as the light was now at his back, she could feel the intensity of his concentration. "What aren't you telling me?" she asked.

He didn't answer. A chill snaked up her spine.

"Does this have to do with your babysitter? Did you talk to the police? Has anyone heard from her?"

"You're cold," he said. "Let's go inside."

Although she knew it wasn't the cold that was making her shiver, she kept quiet. Leaving the dark behind, she made her way to the porch, where welcoming lights shining through the windows and the muted voices of the people inside reminded her there were still places people called home. Maybe not for her, but at least for the children and for Trip, and that thought brought a dollop of comfort. Maybe for an hour or so she could share their homecoming, she could pretend it included her, too.

She could be safe.

And then she would have to return to her basement apartment where David Lee had a key.

TRIP NEVER ENTERED THE ranch house without experiencing a half-dozen simultaneous emotions, all of which were unwelcome tonight. The place held way too much baggage.

What he needed was a few minutes to think, but that wasn't going to happen right away. As Mrs. Murphy made a fuss over Faith, he paused by the big oak hall tree located in the foyer, where he hung his jacket on a hook and caught a glance at himself in the old mirror. He looked pissed. Well, hell, he *was* pissed. He tried a smile. That just made him look worse.

He dug out his cell phone and called the sheriff's department, using the number he'd programmed into the phone several months earlier. The sheriff took down the location of Faith's wrecked car and said to give him a while. Then he called his former boss at the FBI and left a message asking the SAC to include local law enforcement in updates about Neil Roberts.

He took off his gun and holster next and, opening the closet to his right, worked the safe combination and deposited the firearm inside. The safe was one of the very few things he'd brought with him from his old life to his new one. He detoured into the office, spent a few minutes on the Internet, then shuffled through the stack of invoices George had left for him to take care of, while the printer spewed out a dozen images of Neil Roberts. After that, he went looking for Faith and the kids, almost positive where he'd find them.

Mrs. Murphy, his housekeeper, had herded everyone into the big ranch-style kitchen. He was greeted by the smell of beef stew bubbling in a huge cast-iron pot atop the stove and the warmth of a flickering fire in the grate. This was his favorite room in the house, the room that always seemed to wrap its arms around you on a cold night.

Faith sat on a wooden chair with Colin in her lap, while Mrs. Murphy examined the baby head to toe, clucking and fussing as she did so. The little boy had a yellowish knot on his forehead the size of a quarter and wore only a diaper.

Mrs. Murphy looked up from her task and zeroed in on Trip. "Did you find out anything about G-I-N-A?"

Trip shook his head, willing himself not to glance at Noelle.

"Tell me the truth now, was this accident connected to her disappearance?" Mrs. Murphy persisted.

"I can't see how… I just don't know," Trip said. He turned to Noelle then. She sat on a chair by the fire, her solemn gaze taking in everything and everyone as usual. It was hard to believe she was the same screaming, crying child as an hour before, the same little girl who had wrapped her arms around his leg and held on for dear life. It was the first time she'd spontaneously responded to him. He was just sorry it had taken being scared to death to bring her around.

He went to his niece and gently tilted her head back while looking into her eyes. He could find no sign of a concussion.

"What's wrong, Uncle Trip?" Noelle whispered as he rotated one of her small arms and then the other, looking for a sign that something hurt. When she winced, he pushed up the sleeve of her pink T-shirt to find a bruise on her forearm. He pressed it and she flinched a little, but not much.

"What do you mean?"

"Why did Mrs. Murphy spell Gina's name? Where is Gina? Why didn't she come to play with me and Colin?"

"I don't know," he said honestly. "She may have gone off on a little camping trip."

Her voice grew very soft as she said, "Did she bring Buster back first?"

Buster? He shook his head as Mrs. Murphy grumbled, "Camping? In this weather?"

"Chief Novak thinks she went south with her

boyfriend," Trip said, releasing Noelle's arm and turning to his housekeeper.

"Chief Novak, the imbecile," Mrs. Murphy snorted, dismissing the man.

"I don't think Gina liked Peter anymore," Noelle said.

Mrs. Murphy shot Noelle a frown. "Has that girl been babbling on about improper things?"

"No," Noelle said.

Trip doubted Noelle had the slightest idea what "improper things" meant. Nevertheless, his niece's lips slipped in and out of a shy smile. Sometimes the little girl looked so much like her mother that Trip had to glance away to catch his breath. When he did so this time, he found Faith looking away from him as though embarrassed to have been caught watching.

"Nothing wrong with you a good dinner and a hot bath won't cure," he told Noelle. "That and one of Mrs. Murphy's world-famous chocolate cookies," he added, wondering why Faith and Noelle grinned at each other.

"The wee one is fine, too," the housekeeper announced. Faith began dressing the baby again as Mrs. Murphy turned her attention to putting food on the table. The housekeeper eventually attempted to settle Colin in his high chair, but the baby had a stranglehold on Faith's blouse and wasn't letting go anytime soon. Mrs. Murphy wisely backed off.

Dinner was a tense affair. As usual, George Plum joined them, but instead of going over ranch business, everyone ate in stiff silence, because discussing the things they wanted to talk about—the chase, Gina's absence—didn't seem like a good idea in front of Noelle.

There were damn few details to consider, Trip realized as he chewed on a piece of crusty bread he dipped into his stew. Everything was so vague. There was nothing he could pin down, nothing he was sure about except that Gina was missing and Faith had been chased. Period.

He turned to Faith and found her staring at the big black window behind the sink, as though afraid it was about to shatter and let in a thousand demons. He had to know more about David Lee. And he wanted to know what had made her abandon their original plan and drive out to the ranch.

George finally spoke up. "Hal Avery is threatening to quit."

Trip put down his fork. "He's got a background in agriculture. We need him."

"I know. Plus, if he goes, so will his brother, Paul."

"Paul. Tall guy, red hair, good with pneumonia and scours?" Trip asked.

"Yep. The boy knows his way around animals."

"Well, we need him, too. What does Hal want?"

"More money," George replied.

"Give it to him."

"If we give him a raise, then Paul will want one and then Duke and all the rest."

Trip sighed. It didn't matter that running a ranch had never been his idea of a dream job, he was in charge now, like it or not. "Is Duke still off the sauce?"

"Dry as a puddle in late August, far as I can tell. He's a damn good mechanic."

"Then if everyone is willing to settle for a modest increase, go for it," Trip said.

"How much?"

"Modest," Trip snapped. He took a deep breath and added, "You figure it out, okay?"

George patted his pocket, apparently feeling for the reassuring outline of his pipe, and grumbled, "Okay, yeah, sure. You get around to writing the checks for those invoices yet?"

"Later," Trip grumbled as he pushed his plate away. Thinking of Neil Roberts, he added, "George, I want you around when we talk with the sheriff."

"Yeah, okay. Listen, how about the auction on Saturday? They've got a Hereford bull listed. We could use new breeding stock. Do you want me to go, or do you want to do it?"

"You do it," Trip said. Turning to the house-keeper he added, "Mrs. Murphy, your dinner was delicious as usual."

She fluttered a little as she picked up his plate.

"You want I should take care of Buttercup tonight?" George asked.

"The sheriff isn't due for awhile, I'll do it myself," Trip said. He got up and went to the back door. As he pulled on a coat and his hat, he looked at Faith. It was clear she'd given up trying to eat and was now just trying to stay ahead of the mess Colin was making as he banged his spoon against her plate. "Miss Bishop, would you mind coming with me out to the horse barn so we can talk a little before the sheriff gets here?"

Her gaze darted to the window, but she stood abruptly. "Of course I'll come."

She handed Colin to Mrs. Murphy, then leaned down and whispered something in Noelle's ear that brought a smile to the little girl's lips.

Trip tossed her a heavy work coat off a hook by the back door and she shrugged it on. It swamped her, but she gamely zipped it to her chin. The ex-pression on her face as she preceded him through the door was that of a woman facing something she was terrified of.

Chapter Four

Faith glanced up at an overhead fixture to find snowflakes swirling through the stream of light. They melted the second they hit the ground. She bundled the large coat closer to her body, glad she'd worn boots to work that morning. Was it really possible only twelve hours had passed since she'd dressed for work?

The wind blew nearby branches against an outbuilding. A loose chain clattered against a metal post. She glanced around the well-lit yard but found little solace in the shadows creeping in from the vast pastures surrounding the house.

When she'd been attacked before, it had come out of nowhere with no provocation. She didn't even remember the impact of the speeding car and when she'd learned the identity of her assailant it had meant little to her. She hadn't experienced the same degree of fear she'd experienced tonight.

"Faith?"

She'd stopped walking—she was standing in the middle of the yard and Trip was almost to the horse barn. She trotted to his side, embarrassed by her lapse. He must think she was a nutcase.

"It looks like you're building something over there," she told him, pointing at some new construction she'd noticed near one of the outbuildings. She kind of hoped Trip might assume she'd been studying it.

"They started rebuilding the barn that burned down a few months ago, and then thought better of it," Trip explained. "In the spring, we'll tear down what's there and plant the area."

He was talking about the fire that had killed his sister and her husband. "It was so close to the house," she said. "Where were Noelle and Colin?"

"With my brother-in-law's family. You must be freezing, come on."

The welcome shelter of the barn seemed to wrap her in its arms and she relaxed a little. "Who is Buttercup?"

"My sister's horse." At the sound of his voice, a gold horse with a buff-colored forelock and mane tossed her head over the half-open door of her stall and whinnied.

"Is she your horse now?"

He smiled as he looked down at Faith. He had a good face and a good smile. A great mouth. Hard not to speculate what that mouth would feel like against hers. Warmth spread inside at the thought of finding out.

A long pause was broken as he said, "How would it look for a manly guy like me to ride around on a cute little palomino named Buttercup?"

"Pretty silly," she said softly.

"Exactly." When his hand slid along the horse's lovely neck, her own flesh quivered. Buttercup sniffed the brim of his hat as he added, "I'll teach Noelle to ride her in the spring."

Faith touched the horse's velvety nose and was treated to an warm exhalation of breath that caught her off guard. She looked up at Trip again and found him studying her, and tensed as the silence between them stretched like a quivering thread.

He finally walked across the passage and entered an unoccupied stall, returning a second later with a cut of hay and a can filled with grain. He opened the gate and moved inside, the horse following him like a huge yellow puppy, deep rumbles of anticipation in her throat as Trip slid the hay into the rack and deposited the grain in a wall-mounted feeder.

A second later, he was fastening the gate behind him, his gaze once again on Faith. Her hand moved to her cheek, and then her hair, as she glanced down at the hay-strewn dirt floor.

"Aren't there other horses, like for the cow-hands?" she asked.

"They're in a different horse barn down nearer to the ranch house. This barn houses the family's animals, more like pets." He touched Faith's hand and added, "It's getting late—we have to talk."

At his touch, a quiver of recognition jumped through her skin. "Okay."

He leaned against the nearest wall, crossing his arms. "Tell me about David Lee."

Faith rubbed her forehead, closing her eyes for a second. The jolt of the crash hadn't caused any specific injuries, but as time went on she felt increasingly stiff and sore. The last thing she wanted to do was talk about David Lee. "He's my land-lady's son," she finally said. "I went home today to find that his dear old mom gave him a key of his very own. He was inside my place, doing repairs."

"He has a key?"

"What's hers, she says, is his."

"And he was in there without your permission?"

"Yes, and that's not so bad—I mean, he was doing repairs. It's the way he acted, all pushy and entitled. Anyway, that's why I was driving your niece and nephew back here. I had to get away."

"What did he say that made you think he was the one who tried to run you off the road?"

Faith thought back to the confrontation with David and his mother and didn't know how to phrase her misgivings. Time and the subsequent car chase had dulled the impressions of the brief meeting. Maybe she'd just been supersensitive to his remarks because she'd been with Noelle and Colin and felt responsible for them.

"You're second-guessing yourself," he said, taking one of her hands into his. She stared at their joined hands, hers small and pale, his large with the ruddiness of a man who worked outdoors. Did he have the slightest idea what thoughts his touch engendered or of the way he affected her? Was there really something hovering between them or was it all in her head?

"First impressions were bad, I take it," he prompted.

"Yes. But maybe it was me."

"Why do you say that?"

How did she admit she lived in a dump and that it had seemed twice as bad when she saw the dark, cheerless rooms through Noelle's eyes? She shook her head, casually withdrawing her hand and shoving it in a pocket. "The point is, I have no proof it was David. It's a gut feeling. I mean, no one would want to hurt your niece and nephew and I don't have any enemies, especially not in Shay. David thought I rebuked him."

"Did you?"

"Absolutely."

They both turned their heads as a car drove up outside, light from its headlamps sweeping the doorway.

"That has to be Sheriff Torrence," he said, straightening up.

"Wait. When we first got to the ranch, I got the impression you thought you knew who did this."

"Yeah, well, I had a gut reaction, too, just like you did," he replied.

"Who were you thinking of?"

He put a finger against her lips, his touch unexpected. He dropped his hand almost at once, leaving a tingling sensation behind. "Faith," he said softly, drawing her name out as though tasting it.

She whispered, "Yes?"

His dark eyes absorbed her, but she could tell he was backing away from saying whatever had propelled him to murmur her name. *Thank goodness.* She turned, but he caught her arm and she turned again to face him.

"Do you feel it, too?" he asked, his voice very soft, his dark eyes darker than ever, drawing her in.

Shaking inside, she said, "Feel what? No. I don't feel anything—"

In the next instant, he lowered his head. She

knew what was coming. She told herself to back away. She told herself to turn her head.

But she felt powerless to do anything but stay in the moment.

His lips landed on hers with a fiery sputter of lust that shot through her body like a firecracker. In another instant, he'd lifted her from her feet and she'd grasped his muscular arms. His mouth opened, his tongue explored hers, and she reveled in the sensations he evoked. Passion shot sparks through her body, her pulse pounded in her veins, fear and cold vanished.

A car door slammed out in the yard. There were voices.

They broke apart, staring at each other until Trip set her down on her feet again. She couldn't take her eyes from his face, she could barely believe what had just happened.

"Let's go," he said. She sidled past him, happy to escape back into the blowing snowflakes, the black night suddenly less terrifying than her own heart.

SHERIFF BOB TORRENCE was a sturdy man who stood a good foot shorter than Trip. He took off his cap when he entered the house, his shaved head all but reflecting the colored Christmas lights strung across the arch leading into the living area.

"Let me take your coat," Trip said. Torrence

shrugged off the wool jacket with the embroidered emblem on the chest. The sheriff's shoulders were massive, stuffed into a dark brown shirt tucked into jeans. Boots with two-inch heels helped compensate for his short stature. He appeared to have the same coiled energy as Trip.

George Plum joined them in Trip's study, a room filled with business equipment, computers and books. Framed pictures of grazing pastures and snowcapped mountains lined the walls and model train engines in glass cases occupied every spare shelf. A large gun cabinet in one corner held a small arsenal, while a cabinet in another corner held a collection of what appeared to be salt and pepper shakers and oriental fans.

The room didn't fit Trip, at least Faith didn't think it did. For that matter, nothing in the house fit Trip. The kitchen was frilly, the living room done in floral prints, the wallpaper heavy on garlands. She caught a glimpse of a family portrait on a shelf. A big blond man held a younger Noelle, a pregnant woman who looked a lot like Trip at his side. Obviously, the photo was of Trip's sister and her husband, and this house was still theirs in every way that counted but one—they were dead.

After concise but very thorough introductions, Faith was asked to tell her story yet again. No new details came to mind as she spoke.

"Did you get a look at the license plate?" the sheriff asked.

"I tried, but it was dark."

"The light by the plate must have burned out or been smashed somewhere along the way, maybe when he crashed into Faith's car," Trip said.

The sheriff nodded, peering once again at Faith. "Did you notice the color of the plate?"

"I got the impression it was light colored, but that's all."

"Washington, Oregon and California all have white plates," Trip said. "Plus there are vanity plates available in a rainbow of colors."

"And the truck?" the sheriff persisted. "What color was it?"

"Navy or black, I think. Dark. It may have been a van. Not one of the sleek models. A utility type, you know, higher off the ground, like a truck. And older."

"Could you tell if there was more than one person in the vehicle?" Trip asked.

"Not really. Again, just an impression, but I didn't see a passenger."

"Did the lights come out of nowhere?" Trip again.

"No, I think the vehicle was back there for a while, waiting, maybe, for me to get off the main highway. I can't be sure."

The sheriff re-took control of his meeting by clearing his throat. "I'll have your car towed into the station and give it a once-over. Maybe we'll get lucky with a paint sample. Do you have any idea who could have been behind the wheel?"

He fixed her with his light gray eyes. She was about to shy away from mentioning David, until she realized she'd already told Trip about him. It was too late now to have second thoughts about the wisdom of incurring David's wrath, but there wasn't a doubt in Faith's mind he would be livid when he found out he'd been fingered as a suspect.

"The only person I know who seems annoyed with me is my landlady's son, David Lee. I got the impression he's moved back in with his mother."

"There's something else you should know," Trip said as he moved around to the printer at the back of his desk. He picked up a stack of papers and handed one to George and the sheriff before moving over to Faith. His hand brushed hers as he gave her a copy, and she looked up to meet his gaze, once again jolted by his touch, no matter how casual.

His lips twitched when he looked at her, a hint of what had passed between them minutes before lingering in his glance. Warmth spread through her as she watched him return to the desk, but it dissipated in a flash when she looked down at what he'd handed her.

A man. Craggy face, large nose. Short black hair, small black eyes, tall and lanky. He was dressed in an orange jumpsuit, wrists cuffed in back, a squad of faceless lawmen surrounding him as they all walked along what appeared to be a corridor.

With a single glance, she knew this man was a world apart from the David Lees of the world. David was a bully, a creep, but the man in the photo personified evil. He had a mad glint in his hard eyes, an aura of superiority in the set of his shoulders.

"Who is he?" Faith asked, and she heard her voice crack.

"His name is Neil Roberts. I received word he escaped yesterday during a prison transfer, killing one man in the process. Roberts killed four women he abducted from their homes or cars. The last time, he got himself a partner. It took me a year, but in the end we got him right before he was set to strike again."

"But why you?"

"I was the one who figured out who he was. I'm the one who caught him before he killed his last victim."

"Then you take this seriously?" Sheriff Torrence asked. "I mean, that he might come after you?"

"Absolutely. My old boss called to warn me.

He's not a man given to histrionics. We never caught the man Roberts teamed with—he got away. If Roberts somehow meets up with his old pal, well…"

"Where was this Roberts when he escaped?" George Plum asked.

"California. So, yes, he's had time to get here, but it seems unlikely he would have had time to identify and target someone close to me." He addressed Sheriff Torrence. "I don't know if Chief Novak alerted your office, but our babysitter went missing today."

"And you think the car chase, the escape and the missing babysitter are linked?"

"Not necessarily," Trip said. "But that's why I asked George to join us." He flipped a finger at the print in his hand and added, "George, I want this picture shown to everyone who works here in any capacity. Tell them all to keep an eye out, but not to approach him if they see him." He turned back to the sheriff. "We'll take extra precautions until I hear Roberts has been apprehended."

"I'll show the picture to my staff," Sheriff Torrence said. "And what's this about the babysitter? Who is she? The same little gal who worked here before the fire?"

"Yes, my sister hired her a month or two before she died. Her name is Gina Cooke. She didn't show up for work today and her car was found abandoned in town." Trip exhaled sharply. "Chief Novak thinks she's gone off with a boyfriend named Peter Saks. I'll feel better when they track her down, but I have to admit I have no proof anything is related."

"What does your gut tell you?" the sheriff asked, his voice low and quiet.

Trip looked at Faith, then back at the sheriff. "That something is going on. I just don't know what."

Well, Faith thought as the men discussed contingency precautions, *so much for feeling safe at the ranch.*

Safety was an illusion, who should know that better than she?

Okay, as much as she dreaded seeing David Lee, getting in the way of a cold-blooded killer sounded way worse. That meant *she'd* have to deal with David. Maybe she'd stop by the store on her way home and buy some kind of lock she could install on the inside of her apartment door. It wouldn't keep anyone out when she wasn't at home, but it would when she was asleep at night.

"Faith?"

She looked up to find Trip standing over her. The other men were walking out of the study. As tempted as she was to stay and investigate what had transpired out in the barn, she knew she should

leave. Trip was the kind of guy to take responsibility hard. She knew the type well, her brother
was of the same ilk. If she wasn't careful, she'd end
up with another strong-willed man looking out
after her. No, thanks. She was sick of being a
victim. She hadn't moved here for that. She had
two good feet.

Use them to walk away. Use them to stand alone.

She broke eye contact and got up from the
cozy chair. "I'd like to say goodbye to the
children if they're still awake, and then I'll drive
myself home—"

The words hadn't left her lips before she remembered she didn't have a car. *She didn't have a car!*
Insurance wouldn't cover a replacement. What was
she going to do while she waited for a settlement?
The school was five miles from her apartment in a
city with no bus system to speak of.

Why hadn't this occurred to her until now? Had
she blocked it out?

The sheriff ducked his head into the room. "Miss
Bishop? May I take you somewhere? I don't
suggest you go back to your place tonight, not until
we have a chance to talk to your landlady's son.
Maybe your parents or a friend."

"You said you saw my car. Is it, well, drivable?"

He looked surprised she'd even ask such a crazy
thing, and her heart fell. "That bad?" she mumbled.

"It's totaled. I thought you knew. I couldn't believe you and the kids walked away from it pretty much unscathed. That was some fancy driving, Miss Bishop."

That was dumb luck, Faith thought.

"About that ride…"

"I don't know anyone in Shay."

"How about a motel?"

"No." She hadn't meant to blurt it out like that. The fact was, she couldn't afford a motel. "No, thanks, I'll be fine. But I would appreciate a ride back to my place." Maybe she could nail the door shut tonight.

"She'll stay here," Trip said. He looked down at Faith and added, "If you want, of course. The house is huge, you can sleep in the room next to Noelle's. It's up to you."

She tossed a mental coin. Go back to the Lee house and take her chances with David. Stay here and take her chances with a serial killer.

Her gaze lingered on the locked gun cabinet, and then she looked up at the former FBI agent who looked down at her, confidence oozing out his pores, sex appeal trumping the confidence in spades.

Oh, man, she was as good as lost.

So, which was it to be? Fight off her attraction to Trip or her fear of David?

"Well?" Trip probed.

Faith's gaze landed on the framed photo of the shattered family on the bookcase, and something shifted. This wasn't just about her, this was also about Colin and Noelle. "If you're sure it's okay, I'll stay for tonight," she said tentatively. Maybe she'd have the opportunity to talk to Noelle and help her deal with what had been a frightening experience for both of them.

The sheriff had been staring at her, seeing who knew what. Now he said, "You know, Miss, this whole thing may have nothing whatsoever to do with your landlady's son or some escaped felon. We've had trouble with kids out this way before, playing games until it gets out of control." He shrugged. "Could be a bunch of them got liquored up and piled into a van, driving around until they found a lone car to terrorize. The fact that it was driven by a pretty girl would have been a bonus. When you went off the road, they might have gotten scared and taken off."

Faith understood he was offering this as a less-disturbing possibility than the other two scenarios. Strangely enough, it kind of was. She flashed him a high-wattage smile. "Maybe you're right. Maybe it did happen that way."

But she didn't believe it for a moment.

Chapter Five

Thanks to the ever-efficient Mrs. Murphy, the children had been put to bed by the time Trip showed Faith to her room, which was the old master suite.

"It's huge," she said. "Why don't you use it?"

"Too frilly," he said as he looked around at velvet chairs and ruffled curtains.

"You could change it."

"When Mrs. Murphy suggested we move Colin closer to her room so she could tend him during the night, I bunked down in his old nursery. It suits me fine."

"Is your suitcase still packed?"

He ignored her teasing. "Mrs. Murphy said if you'd take her what you need washed, she'll run a load and have it ready in the morning." He gestured at a gown and robe lying across the chair. They must have belonged to his sister. "It looks like she set out a few things for you."

She sat on the edge of the mattress. He couldn't stop looking at her. When her hand flew to her cheek and then to her hair, he gathered his perusal made her nervous. He sat down next to her. "Do you mind if I ask how you got the scars?"

She looked shocked, he supposed at the bluntness of his question, but he let it stand without qualification. "I was attacked last year," she finally said.

"A knife?"

"No. A man tried to kill me by aiming his car at me and stepping on the gas pedal. The cuts came from shattered glass."

Coming from the life he'd led, where he'd heard a thousand worse things and seen the results of even more, he knew this shouldn't rattle him. But it did. "Did you know him?" he asked.

Her answer was a moment coming. "Not really. I'd met him. But I hadn't known his true identity. He didn't hurt me because he hated me or anything. He hurt me to get to my best friend, to frighten her." Bitterness flickered in her eyes. "My brother is a sheriff up in Westerly. He says it was an impersonal crime."

"No crime is impersonal, not if you're the victim," he said, gently grazing a finger down the scar that ran across her cheek.

She shuddered.

"I'm sorry," he murmured.

Casting him an upward glance from beneath her lashes she said, "No one ever touches them. They're ugly."

"There isn't one ugly thing about you," he said, surprised at how much he meant it. "Anyway, they're hardly noticeable." He took a chance and planted a kiss on top of the smallest scar, and again she winced.

"Is that why you limp, too?"

"Yes. I'm mostly recovered, though."

"The car chase tonight must have scared the daylights out of you."

"The thought I might be responsible for getting the children hurt was the worst part."

"Managing your regrets is even trickier," he said.

"Are you thinking of Noelle and Colin?"

"Yes," he said quickly.

She tilted her head as she stared at him. "No, you aren't."

"Faith—"

"Admit it. You're talking about the bus, aren't you? You're thinking about the woman you couldn't get out in time."

"So, now you're a mind reader?" he joked, but she'd nailed him, and he could tell by the wise glint in her eyes that she knew it.

"You got everyone else out," she said softly.

"From what I heard, many of them would have died if you hadn't been the first on the scene."

He'd told himself this a dozen times. To her, he said, "True."

"You don't sound very sure."

He met her gaze and decided to try a few words of raw honesty, see how they felt. "Turning away from that one woman as she begged for help is something I'll never forget. I may have helped save some of the others who might not have made it on their own, but I let her down."

"That's being pretty hard on yourself."

He didn't respond. So much for the truth setting a man free.

"Was she young, old…?"

"Middle-aged, I guess. She had kids, I think, lived over near the pass. She was a large woman, pinned tight. When the explosions started…" He stopped talking and shook his head. "I don't usually talk like this. What happened, happened."

"And you should be tough enough to cope, right?"

"Right."

"If it were just that easy," she mused.

They sat there a moment, wrapped in their own thoughts, closer for having shared and yet a little awkward, too. He finally said, "I'll give you a lift tomorrow morning."

"That would be nice." She licked her lips, probably because they were dry, but the action of her tongue slipping across her mouth immediately captured his attention. His last few affairs had been with women just as beautiful as Faith, just as charming, maybe a touch more worldly. No one since moving—there hadn't been time. He'd had a ranch to reacquaint himself with and two children to attend. Not to mention the staff, the ranch hands, the house personnel…the babysitter. Pieces of lives interrupted and left to him to sort out.

He still didn't have time for any kind of a deep relationship but these things didn't always come on schedule, like a plane or a bus. Faith was here now… She was lovely. He might be pretty good at controlling his impulses, but his imagination had a mind of its own.

"You're off somewhere," she murmured.

He picked up her hand from where it rested on the quilt. "What is it about you, Faith Bishop?"

"I don't know what you mean," she said, but he thought she did.

"In a perfect world, I'd go lock that door and make love to you," he said.

"Would I have a say in it?" she asked wryly.

"Absolutely."

"Well, then, in a perfect world, I'd race you to the door to see who got there first to turn the lock."

She instantly looked surprised by her own words. Before she could take them back, he touched her lips with his own. Her momentary hesitation was gone in a blink. Holding the sides of her head, her hair like silk beneath his fingers, he gently kissed every part of her face he could reach.

She returned the favor, her warm, wet mouth touching his ears and chin and brow, awakening every corpuscle in his body, with a heavy concentration down in his loins. The thrum of her heart beat beneath the pads of his thumbs as he caressed her neck. He wanted to peel her out of her clothes, as she grew softer and warmer with each passing second.

She twisted away from him. Her breathing sounded labored as she rested her forehead against his shoulder. "It's not a perfect world," she murmured.

He ran his fingers down a strand of her golden hair and whispered, "I noticed."

"Trip, I can't do this with you."

"Is there someone else?" he asked huskily.

She looked up at him. "No."

"Then explain it to me. If you're scared of Neil Roberts—"

"It's not Neil Roberts. It's me. I can't explain it all, but I guess the bottom line is I don't want anyone worrying about me."

"It's too late for that," he whispered.

"Don't say that."

"I can't help caring for you, Faith."

For a second she was utterly silent, and then she murmured, "Don't you understand? Your caring for me is a burden I don't need or want."

Her words hung suspended between them. He pulled back a little, not surprised to find her eyes glistening.

"I guess you can't be any more frank than that," he said, looking down at her. He didn't recall getting to his feet, but there he was, standing.

"Trip—"

"I'm curious, though. Why did you say you'd race me to the door?"

"Just because you want something doesn't mean you should take it."

"Not even when it's offered?"

"Not even then. I'm sorry."

He tried out a devil-may-care smile. "It's okay. No damage done. I need to go take care of those invoices anyway." He sighed. "Listen, I'm on the other side of Noelle's room if you need anything. Mrs. Murphy and Colin are at the end of the hall, although I suspect Mrs. Murphy is still downstairs."

She walked to the door with him, he suspected so she could lock it behind him. His desire to pull her into his arms and kiss away whatever was holding her back was so strong he had to think about placing one foot in front of the other. At the door he paused, about to say good night, when she rushed past him into the hall, obviously listening for something. He went into instant alert mode and reached for his gun, but he wasn't wearing one.

For one blinding second, his mind flashed back to the pictures of the women Roberts had abducted and subsequently killed. Images of the woman he'd saved just hours before her death, the suffering they'd all endured. He saw their wounds, felt their despair.

Not again!

"I think it's Noelle," she said, and before he could stop her, she stepped next door and pushed open the child's door. He was right behind her, reaching for her, ready to shield her from harm whether she liked it or not.

The room was softly lit by a night-light and except for the child in one of the twin beds, it was empty, the window closed, peaceful. His heart had been about to burst right out of his chest, but it thudded and skidded to a stop now, falling like a burned-out engine after a rocket launch.

Meanwhile, Faith had pulled a chair to the side of Noelle's bed and perched on the edge.

"What is it, honey?" Faith asked.

He saw the gleaming white of Noelle's eyes as she sniffed. "Buster," she whispered forlornly.

"Buster?"

"Gina said she'd bring him to me. Why didn't she come back?"

Faith looked up at Trip. He shook his head—but then he recalled Noelle had asked about Buster right before dinner. "Who is Buster?" he asked, leaning over Noelle, his hand propped on the back of the chair in which Faith sat.

"He's my polar bear," Noelle said, sniffing back tears.

"Are you sure Gina has him?" He looked at the other bed. It was stacked with stuffed animals.

"Yes—"

"How big is he?"

Noelle's hands came out from under the covers. She held her fingers together, making a circle the size of a softball.

"Why did Gina take him?" he asked.

"I tore his ear," Noelle mumbled into her blankets. "Gina said she'd take him home and sew him back together so his stuffing wouldn't come out."

"Buster is special to you," Faith said gently.

"Mommy gave him to me. Before."

No need to ask before what. Before the fire, before Trip came, before everything changed forever.

"What does he look like?" Trip asked, ready to

tear into the pile of stuffed animals in case Noelle was mistaken.

"He has a purple ruffle and big black eyes."

Trip didn't touch the pile. His mind flashed back to Gina's car and a white-and-purple something stuck between the seat and the back.

"Did Gina know Buster was special to you?" Trip asked.

Noelle nodded.

"Okay, I tell you what. I know just where Buster is, but it's too late to get him tonight. How about you go to sleep and I'll find him for you tomorrow? Can you sleep one more night without him?"

"Okay," she said with a quiver in her voice.

As Faith soothed his niece, Trip grew silent in thought. Would Gina have left something that precious to Noelle in an abandoned car? There was no way to tell for sure, but his instincts said she wouldn't.

It didn't matter what Chief Novak thought, or Gina's mother, either. He was more certain than ever: someone had intercepted Gina.

Chapter Six

George Plum shattered the peace of the morning by storming into the kitchen, swearing and slapping his hat against his leg.

"There'll be none of that," Mrs. Murphy said, pointing a big chef's knife at him. She'd been slicing fruit for the children who sat at the table, oblivious to George's profane bluster.

George apologized, properly cowed. He plopped down across from Trip. "Duke Perry didn't show up for work and he isn't answering his phone."

"What about Hal and Paul?"

"I offered them five percent. They seem content enough, at least for now, but we need Duke. The tractor is dead in the water and the cows down in the east pasture need feed." He grimaced. "We're supposed to get a foot of snow next week, hell, we were out there this morning, breaking ice on the water troughs. I'm going into town to Duke's place to see if he fell off the wagon and is sleeping one off."

"How about the photo? Did you show it around?"

"Not yet."

Not yet. George's priority was feeding cows, not keeping killers at bay. Trip went back to the den and got a few copies, then went outside with George. They found Hal and Paul and a handful of other hands in the machine shop staring at the dead tractor, drinking coffee and stamping their feet against the cold.

Trip handed out the photos and the warnings, assigned one of the men to keep a close eye on the house for the day, then pulled aside the younger of the Avery brothers. After he had enlisted Paul's aid, Trip went back inside to find Noelle waiting for him, her backpack slung over her thin shoulders. Faith stood at the counter downing coffee.

"Ready to go?"

Noelle finished her juice, then Faith buttoned her coat up to her chin and pulled on a knit cap she fished from her pocket. For the tenth time since seeing her that morning, he acknowledged wanting her like he'd never wanted anyone before.

Had it ever happened this fast before? Lust, sure. But this other thing, this desire just to be near a woman?

As Colin threw cereal all over the kitchen, Trip paused by Mrs. Murphy and lowered his voice.

"Don't let the baby out of your sight today. And please, if you don't mind, stay inside."

A shadow crossed the housekeeper's face as she nodded at him.

Recalling how she'd shuddered after he'd shown her the picture of Neil Roberts, he had a feeling she'd barricade herself and Colin behind locked doors without complaint. "If Gina doesn't show up today I'll find someone else to watch Colin," he added.

"Be off with you," she scolded. "The wee one and I will get along nicely, just go catch that dreadful man."

He felt like saluting.

Instead, he ushered Noelle and Faith out to the truck. Within a half hour, he was at the school, letting them both off near the office.

"Should I keep her here until I go home…" Faith's voice petered out as she apparently realized that after school she'd be stuck. She quickly caught herself and said, "I can get a ride home from another teacher, but I don't want to take Noelle to my place. Ever."

"I'll pick up Noelle. And don't worry about getting home—I have business in town later and will give you a ride."

"No, thanks," she said, her warm exhalations making ghostly shapes around her face, blurring her features for a moment.

"Please, Faith. Maybe I'll have found out something by then that you need to know. You can be as independent as you want tomorrow," he added softly, resisting the urge to grab her shoulders and plant a kiss on her perfect lips.

He could see curiosity steal across her features, at least he assumed that's what it was. She finally nodded, and then he watched as she and Noelle disappeared inside the brick building.

As soon as they were out of sight, he drove around the corner and pulled up behind a blue truck.

SHAY'S DINER AT THE EDGE of town was the unofficial meeting site for half the ranchers in the area. Since returning to Shay, Trip had taken to stopping by after delivering Noelle to school. It was not only a way to get reacquainted with small town life, but also to keep on top of things. Years of always knowing everything made knowing very little hard to swallow.

On this morning, his aim was a lot more important than a little friendly patter. He'd spied the sheriff's car in the parking lot. He took off his hat as he entered the noisy building, nodding at Marnie, the waitress he'd known since grammar school. She'd never left Shay, had stayed and married right out of high school, and now had a son away at college.

Bypassing the group he usually joined, he threaded his way to the back, where he saw Sheriff Torrence and another man at a table for four. He turned when he heard someone in a nearby booth hail him, and found himself looking at the kid from the gas station, Eddie something. No wonder he'd recognized the kid, everyone turned up at Shay's Diner sooner or later. He nodded a greeting before taking a seat across from Sheriff Torrence.

"Trip, you know Fire Chief Tom Gallows, right?" Sheriff Torrence said.

Setting his Stetson on an empty chair, Trip shook Gallows's hand. "Sure. You investigated the barn fire out at the Triple T last September."

With his silver hair and David Niven mustache, Gallows looked more like an aging leading man than a fire chief. "That was a terrible business," he said.

Trip nodded although the worst of it had been cleaned up and hauled away by the time he'd rearranged his life to come back to Shay. Even the construction of a new barn had been started in an attempt to sweep away the past.

Gallows took a sip of coffee as he added, "I kept thinking I'd find traces of foul play, though who would have wanted to hurt Susan and Sam Matthews? Pillars of the community. Real ranchers, those two. Had it in their blood. They were a great couple. Great parents."

"Yes," Trip said. Real ranchers. It was true. Much to their father's chagrin, Susan had always been much more interested in ranching than Trip had. When she'd married Sam, his father had been ecstatic. "They were great," he agreed, and meant it. He put thoughts of his sister and brother-in-law aside and directed a question at Torrence. "Did you talk to David Lee last night?"

"We couldn't find him," Torrence said. "His mother insisted he was off with friends, but she couldn't name the friends. She also claims he doesn't own a van or truck. Says he drives an old white Mercury that used to be hers."

"What does she drive?"

"We thought of that. A yellow coupe."

"Are you heading back there this morning?"

"Of course."

"I want to go to the Lee house with you."

"In what capacity?" the sheriff asked.

"Curious bystander."

Torrence lowered his voice. "Are you carrying?"

"Yes, but that's because of Neil Roberts, not David Lee."

Torrence stared hard at Trip for a moment as Marnie showed up at the table wielding a carafe. She refilled the other two cups as she gestured at Trip's. "What about you, handsome?" she asked Trip.

He smiled up at her. "Marnie, when are you

going to leave that husband of yours and run off with me?"

"He's away on another one of those blasted business trips, so don't tempt me," she teased, with a dazzling smile. "Meanwhile, coffee?"

"No, thanks. I'm trying to sweet-talk the sheriff."

"You always have coffee," she said.

"I know, but not today."

"Okay, honey, you just holler if you change your mind," she said with a wink, then sashayed off to an adjoining table.

Trip looked back at Torrence. "Well?

Torrence shrugged. "Sure, you can tag along. I'm meeting my deputy here in ten minutes."

Fifteen minutes later, Trip trailed the sheriff and deputy to the Lee house, growing more and more surprised as the neighborhoods grew seedier. When Torrence pulled up in front of a single-story white house, he could barely believe his eyes.

From the front, the house appeared to be a single-floor dwelling, but after Trip pulled ahead to park, he saw another level below, with a sharply sloping driveway on the side. There looked to be a garage or workshop at the bottom of the gulley opposite the basement, then the heavily wooded land rose steeply up the other side of the ravine to meet the back of a row of houses. He bet the basement apartment got no direct sunlight.

Trip met the sheriff on the sidewalk, gesturing a half block away at an old white Mercury pulled up to the curb. "Looks like the son's home now," Trip said.

"Goody," Torrence quipped.

The two officers walked up to the front door, oozing purpose, another day at the office. Trip hung back, out of the way. Torrence pounded twice and waited. It took a while, but the door was eventually opened by a haggard-looking woman in her late forties, wrapped in a polyester robe. Despite the early hour, she wore a full face of heavy makeup, including apple-red lipstick and thick black eyeliner.

"He still isn't home," she said.

"His car is here," Torrence said calmly.

"It is? I didn't hear him come in."

"How about letting us take a look around?"

She glanced over her shoulder. Trip was so sure her son was lurking in the room behind her, he ached to kick the door out of her hand. He heard the creak of a floorboard as the landlady turned her attention back to Torrence. She raised her voice and demanded he leave her alone and stop harassing her, her boy hadn't done anything wrong. The deputy rolled his eyes.

Trip stepped off the rotting wood porch. No one

was paying him any attention. As he moved around the side of the house, he heard a door open and close somewhere down below. He pressed himself against the house.

Sure enough, the kid came tearing up the driveway, angling out to reach the sidewalk and his Mercury, apparently oblivious to Trip's presence. At that moment, the deputy came around the front of the house, caught sight of Lee running toward his car and yelled, "Hey, you. Stop!"

Lee paused for a microsecond, then kept going. He was pretty fast on his feet for a walking muscle. Faster than the deputy, anyway. Trip, who had fallen back to let the deputy do his job, now saw the deputy was never going to catch David before he disappeared around the corner and into a labyrinth of back streets and alleys he no doubt knew better than any of them. Trip took off as Lee apparently rethought his plan and darted toward his car.

Out of the corner of his eye, Trip saw the deputy pull a gun. No way. He didn't want David Lee shot—he wanted to know if the bastard had chased Faith the night before. He was afraid the young deputy's inexperience and the heat of the chase would end up in a disaster, so he ran faster. Ruby Lee started yelling encouragements to her wayward son from the front porch.

Lee raced around to the driver's door of his car and tore it open. Trip threw himself across the hood, slid on his stomach, landed on his feet and pushed his shoulder into the door, catching Lee half in and half out.

By now, the deputy had reached them, gun drawn, temper high. More shouting ensued as everyone told everyone else what they thought. Ruby Lee came running, her slippers slapping on the pavement, swearing like a sailor as her house-coat flapped around her legs. Trip pushed himself off the back fender where he'd spun after impact and watched the deputy snap handcuffs on Lee's beefy wrists.

Bottom line, David Lee was unhurt though he threw Trip a glare of pure hatred. Trip had been the recipient of too many baleful stares over the years to quake in his boots with this jerk, but his fists bunched at his sides anyway.

FAITH LOOKED OUT THE window for the fortieth time in an hour. The sky was leaden and heavy looking, forbidding—a perfect reflection of her mood.

Though she sat on a small chair holding a picture book and reciting long-ago-memorized text, every-thing struck her as surreal. Twenty-four hours before, she'd defined the world by different par-ameters. She'd had goals—pay off her bills, be a good teacher, rediscover her trust in the world. She'd had fears, but they'd been drifting away.

Now, in the face of the violence of the past day or so, everything was different. Her leg hurt worse than it had in ages, and so did her damn back and some nameless place deep inside where she'd suffered additional injuries. Over and over again she found her fingers tracing her scars. Though she tried to remember the tender, warm feeling of Trip's fingers and lips, she couldn't.

A little boy seated on the rug closest to her feet opened and closed the Velcro closure on his shoes as he stared up at her, eyes round. Faith snuck a peek at Noelle, who sat off by herself on the edge of the group, dark circles beneath her eyes, pigtails drooping, gaze settled on the hamster cage on the shelf by the window. Was she thinking about her polar bear? Or about the car chase or her parents? How much pain should one child have to endure? Faith caught Noelle's eyes and smiled warmly. The child's lips curved for a moment.

The hall door opened quickly, causing Faith's heart to jam in her throat. One of the secretaries stepped hesitantly inside the room, gesturing at Faith.

"Principal Cooper wants you in the office right now," Paty Jones whispered, her green eyes bright with intrigue.

"My class—"

"I'll stay here with the kids while you're gone."

"Okay," Faith said, handing the secretary the book, her finger holding the place where she'd left off. "Do you know why Principal Cooper wants to see me?"

"They found a suspicious-looking man lurking outside."

Faith swallowed what felt like a five-pound brick of ice. "A man? Who?"

"I don't know."

"What's he got to do with me?"

"I don't know. The principal is ready to call the cops—you better hurry."

Faith walked down the hall, the image of Neil Roberts vivid in her head. What if he'd used some ruse to get inside the school? What if he whipped out a gun the moment Faith entered the office? What if he'd already hurt Principal Cooper?

Her mind told her to stop being an idiot—no one would approach a school this way. It didn't make sense.

She turned the corner into the principal's office to find Principal Geri Cooper standing across the desk from a man Faith had never seen before. He looked to be about thirty, with sandy hair. Tall and thin, he was dressed in jeans, boots and a bulky parka. He held a new cowboy hat in big, rough-looking hands.

Best of all, he was not Neil Roberts.

"Do you know this man?" Principal Cooper asked, peering at Faith over the top of her bifocals.

"No."

"My name's Paul Avery, I work for Luke Tripper out at the Triple T, I told you that," the man said. "Mr. Tripper told me to keep an eye on the school this morning, and I got cold so I walked around the place to see if anyone suspicious was hanging out."

"You were seen walking around the campus three times," Principal Cooper said. "That's what was suspicious."

"I'm used to moving," Paul Avery said. "Don't like sitting much."

"The janitor noticed him," Principal Cooper added as she glanced at Faith. "Do you know what he's talking about?"

Faith recognized the name Paul Avery from dinner conversation the night before. But was this man who he said he was? "Why don't you call Mr. Tripper and ask if he sent him?"

"I tried. His cell phone number isn't answering."

She leveled her gaze at Paul Avery. "Who's the Tripper housekeeper?"

"Mrs. Murphy," he said at once.

"And your brother's name?"

"Which one? Hal works at the Triple T with

me, Jason is still in school and Len is with the 82nd Airborne in Afghanistan."

"I think he's who he says he is," Faith said dryly.

"Hm—" Principal Cooper glowered at Avery. "Why are you watching our school?"

Avery looked at Faith quickly, then away.

"I know why he's here," Faith said. "He's watching over Noelle Matthews. There's been some weird things going on at the ranch, right, Mr. Avery?"

Avery shrugged.

Principal Cooper lowered her voice. "Weird things? Why wasn't I told about this before now?"

"I didn't think trouble would follow anyone to this school," Faith explained.

"What kind of trouble are we talking about?"

"A missing babysitter—"

"Who?"

"Gina something. I can't remember her last name."

"Cooke," Avery said. "Her name is Gina Cooke."

"I know Gina," Principal Cooper said. "She went to this school. What do you know about this, Mr. Avery?"

Paul Avery looked ready to sink into the linoleum. He twisted his hat in his hands as he muttered, "Nothing. Honest. No one was supposed to know I was even here. The boss is going to kill me."

"I wouldn't worry about your boss right now,"

the principal said. "I'd worry about me. If you don't start making sense right now, I'm calling the police. The Chief used to be a student of mine, too. As would you and your brothers have been if you'd lived in this town long enough."

Avery's Adam's apple slid up and down his throat.

"You're here to watch over Noelle, right?" Faith said.

"Well, yeah, but not just her."

"What do you mean?" Principal Cooper snapped.

Avery looked down at his worn boots and shrugged.

Principal Cooper was obviously nearing the end of her patience. "Ms. Bishop, Faith, sit down. Tell me what's going on and how it affects the children in this school. Not so fast, Mr. Avery, you sit down, too."

Paul Avery reluctantly parked himself on the indicated chair. As Faith took the other chair, she looked up at the clock, an uneasy feeling gnawing at her stomach. With Avery and her both in the office it left the classroom vulnerable to an attack by Neil Roberts. She got to her feet.

Principal Cooper looked up.

"I promise I'll come back after school today and tell you everything I know, but please, I have to get back to the classroom. I'd like Mr. Avery to come with me."

Principal Cooper leveled a stare at Avery. "You aren't carrying a weapon, are you?

As Avery pulled a silver object from a coat pocket, Faith's breath caught in her throat and the principal started to rise from her seat. He opened his hand to reveal a cell phone. "Just this, ma'am," he said.

Shaking her head, the principal looked at Faith. "You have some explaining to do. I don't appreciate your leaving me in the dark about security issues."

"It wasn't my intention—"

"There are only three more days until Christmas vacation," the older woman said as she sank back down in her seat. "I, for one, can hardly wait. Okay, go on, go back to class. You, too, Mr. Avery. But be warned, I will call the police if I feel the need. And turn that phone off."

Faith left in a hurry, only vaguely aware that Paul Avery trailed behind her. She had to get back to her class.

She rushed through the door at last, stopping dead in her tracks. But instead of a scene out of a horror movie, she found the children still sprawled on the rug, the secretary perched on the little chair, reading another book. As one, they turned curious eyes to stare at her. Faith's gaze went straight to Noelle, who smiled.

Paul Avery bumped into Faith from behind and she whirled to face him.

"Sorry, ma'am," he muttered.

The ebbing adrenaline rush of the last few moments left Faith's knees weak. What was happening to her?

Damn Luke Tripper.

Chapter Seven

Trip pulled up to the school in the early afternoon. It had been twenty-four hours since the last time he parked in pretty much the same spot. Twenty-four eventful and incredibly frustrating hours.

He was just reaching for his hat when the front door of the school seemed to blow off its hinges. A slightly built blond dynamo emerged, breathing fire, covering the distance from the school to the parking lot in record time, hair loose from the chignon she usually wore.

Uh-oh.

She walked around the truck, opened the passenger door and climbed in, dragging her purse and book bag behind her. For a moment she sat staring out the windshield, her belongings piled in her lap, coat bunched around her legs. Waves of anger filled the cab.

He finally said, "Faith?"

She turned slowly to face him. "What?"

"Is something wrong?"

"Oh, no, nothing is wrong," she huffed. "Well, unless you mean that my principal no longer trusts my judgment. She's not too crazy about yours, either."

He sat back in the seat. "I take it Paul Avery made a mess of things."

"I hope he's better with cows than he is with principals." She dumped all her stuff on the floor by her feet and rubbed her forehead. "It never crossed my mind to fill Principal Cooper in on yesterday's events. I never considered the possibility violence would follow me or Noelle to the school."

"I did," he said.

"I know. But you didn't share your plans with me."

"You didn't want me protecting you."

"So you went around my back?" she snapped.

As that's exactly what he'd done, he sidestepped answering. "Did anything happen today?"

"Besides Paul Avery causing me a boatload of trouble?"

"No sign of—"

"Felonious killers? Nope. But that does not excuse your trying to protect me when I asked you not to. Promise me you won't do something like that again."

"I promise. But about Paul… It's not like I have

the FBI's best agents to draw from, you know. You should never even have known he was around."

"And that would have made your being sneaky okay?"

"I guess not," he admitted.

"He circumnavigated the school three times and scared the janitor," Faith added. "Didn't he call and tell you about this?"

"He just left a message saying Noelle was with him and they were at the ranch and you were fine. I've either been at the sheriff's office, on the phone with the FBI or trying to talk George Plum down off the cliff, because our erstwhile mechanic fell off the wagon last night."

Her eyes shifted uneasily as she said, "The FBI? Did they catch that man?"

"No. But Colby—that's my SAC—said he heard there's an agent in Idaho with a lead on Roberts's old partner."

"Is that good? I mean as far as finding Roberts goes?"

He shrugged. "Maybe…hard to tell."

She reached over her shoulder and snagged the seat belt. "I'm sorry about the mechanic. Take me home, please, and tell me about David Lee."

As he drove out of the lot, he told her about Lee's arrest.

"Then he's in jail?" she said with a relieved sigh.

"Not exactly. He swears he didn't chase you and he doesn't own a truck or a van. The sheriff let him out on bail—he had no choice. That doesn't mean the investigation is over, it just means he's not behind bars."

"But he ran."

"He owes a few hundred dollars in traffic fines. He says he thought he was being arrested for those, hence he panicked."

"Great."

Sheriff Torrence is no fool. He's sure Lee is behind the chase…the jerk couldn't quite keep a smirk off his face. To tell you the truth, I find it kind of comforting."

"And how is that?" she asked.

He spared her a glance as he turned off Main Street and drove over train tracks. "David Lee is a two-bit loser. That doesn't mean he's not danger-ous, but it does mean he's not in the same league as someone like Neil Roberts."

"Yeah, well, meanwhile, David Lee will probably be staying with his mother. If he makes one move toward me, I'm going to punch him."

The spontaneous smile her words evoked from him faded away as he recalled the scorn in Lee's eyes. Taking a deep breath he said, "You have to move out of there."

"Don't be crazy. I'm not leaving."

"Just because Lee isn't a cold-blooded murderer doesn't mean he's not capable of violence. Rape, for instance."

"Don't try to scare me," she warned.

"That's exactly what I'm trying to do. There has to be another apartment in Shay—"

"I can't move, Trip."

"Can't or won't? Don't be stubborn."

"Where do you get off telling me I'm stubborn?" she growled.

He reined in his impatience. He had no right to make demands of her. She wasn't his employee or his lover. She'd told him to back off.

"I'm sorry," she said when he was silent. "I'm the one who called you last night when I was in trouble. I'm the one who asked for help."

"You were scared."

"Tell me about it. But now I'm mad, and I shouldn't take it out on you. Meanwhile, I will not allow a lowlife like David Lee to run me out of my home. I can't believe I just called that hole a home. Anyway, I'll nail the damn door shut first."

"Don't get me wrong, I admire your spunk, but there's also an inside staircase," he said as he maneuvered the big truck through narrow old streets lined with parked cars.

"An inside staircase? You mean from Ruby's house to my apartment?"

"Your apartment used to be the basement, right?"

"Of course, I should have thought of that. But I've never seen a door—"

"It's at the back of a small room, behind a sliding panel next to a little closet full of tools."

"I saw the closet. I didn't know about the panel."

"I didn't think so. It looks as though you didn't use the room for anything other than storing furniture and boxes." For a second he thought about that dark, dank cave. It was hard to picture Faith living there.

"You have to leave," he insisted as he drove down Ruby Lee's driveway and parked in front of Faith's pathetic excuse for a home. "You're in danger here."

"Trip, just stop. I can't afford a move. I paid two months' rent up front plus a nonrefundable cleaning deposit. I have medical bills to pay off if I'm ever going to be solvent again. I need to stay put."

"If they are abusing your rights, they should have to give you a refund."

"I thought of that. Enforcing it is the trouble."

The wind whistled by the truck as he assimilated this news and searched for a way to tell her what he had in mind. It was getting dark outside. She looked at him across the dim interior of the truck.

"Face it, I'm broke. There is no shame living hand to mouth, but I used rotten judgment moving into this dump, and now I'm going to make the best of it."

No way was he leaving her here with David Lee lurking around upstairs. "I have a proposition for you."

She narrowed her eyes.

"Not that kind," he said quickly, but he was secretly pleased she'd made the leap to sex so quickly. Sitting in the half dark, her face a glowing pale oval, her eyes heavily shadowed, she looked ethereal. He wanted her badly, not that wanting her was going to do him any good. He added, "I need a babysitter…you need a place to live and a car to drive to work. You're great with kids—"

"I have a job," she interrupted. "At least, I think I still do."

"Exactly. What, two more days of work and then a couple of weeks of vacation, right? Spend the time at my place. If you don't want to sleep in the house, fine, you can have one of the vacant cabins. The ranch is crawling with unused vehicles this time of year."

"This is very kind of you but—"

"And in return," he said, talking over her, "you help me find a new babysitter. I don't think Gina is coming back anytime soon. I don't know how to hire someone new, and you said you wanted to help Noelle, inside or outside of school."

"Mrs. Murphy can help you."

"Mrs. Murphy will pick someone she approves of, someone solid and respectable and as fun as dirt. I want someone Noelle and Colin like."

Her fingers made the trip past her cheek and into her hair as she considered his offer. "What about us?" she finally said.

"What about us?"

"You know."

"I have no idea what you're talking about."

Her laugh sounded forced. "Okay, we'll pretend 'us' never happened."

"Isn't that what you wanted?" he murmured.

"Yes. And Neil Roberts? Have they caught him yet? Has anyone seen him?"

"No one. He's disappeared. That's another reason I'd like you at the ranch."

"So you can keep an eye on me."

He tried what he hoped was an engaging smile, assuming she could see it. "I'm not allowed to worry about you, I forgot."

"You're impossible," she said.

"Maybe, but maybe I'm just more experienced with things like this."

"I have no desire to put myself in harm's way—"

"Then come to the ranch, save a little money so

you can make a decent move in January, get me through the hiring process for a replacement for Gina. You'd be helping me and the kids."

She looked over her shoulder at the dingy white house and then back at him. "I'd like to help Noelle and Colin."

He noticed how she hadn't mentioned helping him. "Then you'll come?"

"No hovering?"

"Not even if Neil Roberts shows up in Shay?"

"Maybe then," she said.

RUBY LEE SHOWED UP as Faith carried a box out to Trip's truck. By the way she teetered down the drive and stood leaning against the fence, it looked as though she'd started the evening festivities a little early.

She narrowed her eyes when Trip exited through the doorway carrying an armload of clothes still on hangers.

"You!" Ruby screamed.

"Evening," Trip said, depositing the clothes in the backseat of the cab.

"You were with those damn cops this morning," she hissed. Turning her wrath on Faith, she added, "And you're the one who fingered my boy."

"Yes, I admit it, I told the sheriff the only one I

could think of who would try to harm me and two innocent children was your son."

"He would never!"

Faith shook her head. "The sheriff will figure it out. If David is guilty, I'll press charges. If he's not, I'll apologize. Meanwhile, I've decided to move out."

"Good riddance."

"And I want my money back."

"That's outrageous," Ruby said, letting go of the post and grabbing it again when she wobbled. "I rented to you in good faith."

"You and your son have made it impossible for me to live here," Faith said.

Trip cleared his throat. "There's always small claims court—" he began.

Faith glanced at him. "Please," she said. "I'll take care of this." Looking back at Ruby, she added, "Mr. Tripper is right, though."

"You have no proof of anything," Ruby seethed. "And if you want to sue me, go ahead and try."

Faith finally realized she was still holding the heavy box. She plopped it down in the back of the truck and shoved it forward. "Then is it okay with you if I leave a few things in the back room until later? I mean as long as I'm paying rent?"

"Sure," Ruby said, almost gloating. "You're paid up until the end of January—it's yours to do with what you will."

"Thank you."

"I'm a reasonable woman," Ruby said, and then she seemed to realize she'd started this conversation angry with Faith and Trip for getting her beloved son in trouble. She turned unsteadily and lurched her way back up the driveway.

As soon as she was gone, Trip said, "I can have someone come get the rest of your things later tonight. No need for you to stay tied to this dump."

Faith shook her head. "Thanks, Trip, but no." She went back to lock the door behind her, grateful when he let the matter drop.

This time, when they crossed the cattle guard under the Triple T sign, Faith felt a sense of homecoming. She knew it was fantasy, but she didn't care. The very fact she didn't have to worry about running into David Lee made her heart feel lighter. No more drunken diatribes from Ruby, either.

And yet, as they drove up the road she had to admit there were also no locked gates, no guards, nobody to keep someone intent on evil from taking the same road they traveled into the heart of the ranch. And at the heart? The house, of course, warmly glowing with Christmas lights as before, but also the new wood rising from the ashes of a burned out barn, a phoenix soon to be struck down again.

Trip drove past the house, stopping when he reached a small cabin-like structure that sat close to the house on the other side of a fence. It was built up off the ground, with stairs and a broad porch. He turned off the engine and honked the horn a couple of short blasts. Within seconds, a cluster of ranch hands appeared from around the back. They each took a box or two and, as Trip opened up the cabin and switched on the lights, carried the belongings Faith had brought with her inside.

As she walked behind them, carrying an armful of clothes, a sudden gust of chilly wind assaulted her nose. She could swear she smelled the acrid remains of smoke.

The cabin was really just a glorified studio apartment, but it was clean and dry and had obviously been made ready, probably by Mrs. Murphy. There was a poinsettia plant on the counter, along with a stack of folded linens and a few basic supplies. Weak light filtered in through the skylight right above the bed.

"It's not very big—" Trip began, but Faith hushed him.

"It's perfect. It's snug and safe and clean and warm, and best of all, private. Thank you." The fact that she could see the new construction outside the window? Immaterial.

"Wait until my ad goes in the paper and you have to start interviewing applicants for a nanny," he said. The ranch hands, including a very sheepish looking Paul Avery, had departed and now it was just the two of them. Trip looked bigger than ever standing in the small space.

Gesturing toward her little kitchen, which was really an alcove containing a microwave, hot burner, tiny fridge and a toaster, he said, "You're welcome to eat inside with the rest of us."

"I have the food I brought from my old place," she said. "I think I'll stay in tonight and get everything all situated. It's a workday tomorrow."

"Just so you know, you're welcome anytime. Oh, and I'll dig up the keys to a car for you."

"Thanks. I meant to ask about Buster."

"I drove out to Gina's mother's place and asked if I could get him out of Gina's car. She didn't care one way or another. I'll give him to Noelle when I go inside."

"So Gina left Buster in her abandoned car?"

"Yeah. I saw him yesterday."

"Did she sew him up?"

"Good as new."

"If Gina knew the toy was that important to Noelle, would she have gone off and left it like that?"

"I don't think so," he said cautiously, "but who knows for sure. If she was excited about going away with Peter Saks, maybe she just forgot." He glanced at his watch and added, "I'd better get inside."

She followed him to the door in order to lock it after his departure. He turned the knob and the wind tugged on the door, admitting a slap of cold air. She touched his arm and said, "Again, thanks."

He looked down at her, his eyes mysterious beneath the brim of his hat, holding her gaze. He put his hand over hers. She couldn't seem to turn away. It was like they were caught in amber, the cold all but forgotten, nothing existing except the two of them.

"Boss?" The word was immediately followed by an "Er… Oh, sorry…"

Faith came back to reality with a thud, the cold wind snaking through her clothes. A whiff of aromatic smoke tickled her nose as she turned to find George Plum and another man standing on the small porch outside the open door. George was puffing on an ivory-bowled pipe.

The newcomer appeared to be about Faith's age, in his late twenties. He wore dark clothes that looked a little baggy, had a round face and a round-shouldered frame. A wisp of a fair mustache brushed his upper lip.

Trip turned to him. "Eddie, right? I saw you this morning at the diner."

The younger man grinned. "I saw you, too. I'm Eddie Reed, the mechanic."

"Sure," Trip said.

George piped in. "He showed up today."

"I heard old Duke got a snootful at the tavern last night and got himself thrown in jail," Eddie said.

Trip narrowed his eyes. "Where did you hear that?"

"At the diner, where else? Being in the same line of work, me and Duke got lots of the same friends. I figured you was going to be needing a new mechanic so I hightailed it out here."

"He's right, we do," George said.

"Has Duke been charged with anything?"

George plunged his hands in his jacket pockets, as though the cold was getting to him. "This is his third DUI, he ain't getting out of jail anytime soon."

Trip swore. "He knew what was at stake—I warned him often enough. I'm sorry to hear he fell off the wagon, but getting behind the wheel of a car, that's the end of it as far as the Triple T is concerned. Still, I'll go talk to him, make sure we aren't judging him before we get the facts, see what he has to say for himself."

"Then you want I should delay hiring Eddie?"

"Can you give us a day or two?" Trip asked.

Eddie shrugged. "Sure."

"Boss, I hate to disagree with you, but the weatherman is predicting snow and the hay tractor is down," George interjected. "We need Eddie now. If it's okay with you…"

"No offense, Eddie, but we'll need to run background checks before we can make anything permanent."

"No offense taken," Eddie said.

"Couldn't he work now and we'll do that next week?" George asked.

"Yeah, okay, go ahead. Welcome aboard, Eddie," Trip added, extending a hand.

Eddie Reed looked as excited as a small kid on the first day of an adventure as he uttered his thanks.

Trip turned back to Faith. "Are you sure I can't send someone to the Lee house to get the rest of your belongings?"

"I'm sure," she replied.

"If you end up suing her to get your money back, it will look better if you moved out all the way. Asking her to store things—"

"Trip? Let it drop, okay?"

He tugged on the brim of his hat. "I'll leave you to get settled."

As Trip and the other two men walked off, Faith closed the door and turned the lock.

Chapter Eight

It didn't take long to find a place for everything. The last item to be unpacked was the little porcelain figurine that Olivia had insisted Faith keep. Dressed in blue, bowing to an invisible escort, her best friend said it reminded her of Faith because of the blue eyes and yellow hair. Faith didn't see herself in the little doll, but it did remind her of Olivia.

A knock on the door took care of an impending wave of nostalgia by sending her heart into overdrive. There was no way to see who was on the other side, no peephole through which to peek.

Did people like David Lee and Neil Roberts knock on doors, though? She stood rooted to the floor, waiting.

"Faith, it's me. I have news!"

Trip. Almost as dangerous, in his own way, as Lee or Roberts. She opened the door and stood aside. No use pretending she wouldn't let him in.

"Guess what," he said, closing the door. When

he grabbed her arms, the pressure of his fingers raced through her veins. "Colby just called. Neil Roberts was sighted down in San Diego. He must be trying to cross the border into Mexico. We as good as have him."

"That *is* great news," she said, and flung her arms around his neck.

Mistake. She was wearing satin pajamas, and the moment her breasts rubbed against his chest and his hands wrapped around her back, she could feel the sizzle of his desire burn through the slinky material.

Or was it her desire?

She lowered her arms, determined to reestablish boundaries.

His grip loosened, but he kept her within the circle of his arms. She faced the fact it was very comfy there.

"Don't get me wrong," he added. "Until we have the son of a bitch behind bars again, there's no point in letting down our guard. But it looks promising. Roberts has been sighted a thousand miles away, all is right with the world. Except for David Lee, but we'll get him, too."

"This is a side of you I haven't seen," she said, looking up into his glittering dark eyes.

"What do you mean?"

"The happy, carefree side."

"The relieved side, that's all."

"It's very attractive," she said.

He raised his eyebrows.

She started to laugh, but there was something in his gaze that killed the impulse. Something that reminded her how close they were standing, of the weight of his hands touching the top curve of her bottom, of the wide set of his shoulders and his inherent masculinity.

As his fingers flexed against her satin-covered skin, lust shot through her pelvis, bypassing the mended bones and scars and creating a whole new sensation of its own.

One kiss, she thought frantically, willing him to sense her shifting emotions, to free her from the decision to take matters into her own hands. She'd told him she didn't want him caring for her, she didn't want the responsibility of his affection or concern. And she didn't, she really didn't. He'd respected her desires, he'd backed off, and now she was telling him something else, and this time without uttering a single word.

And she meant that, too.

Very slowly, she raised her arms again until they circled his neck, her breasts once again pressing against his chest. His gaze went from her breasts to her eyes, the tension in his big body vibrating through hers, his obvious desire empowering her in unexpected ways. She raised herself on tiptoes, pulling the back of his head just a little—and he lowered his face slowly, giving her all the time in the world to slip away, to change her mind, to come to her senses.

Until his lips touched hers, and then time was up.

The kiss was long and wet and moistened every vulnerable inch of her body, priming her for the erection she could feel growing against her thigh. His desire inflamed her own, and when his hand slid over her rear and down the back of her legs, she all but shuddered with the strength of her need for him. He lifted her into his arms effortlessly, never breaking the connection they'd forged with their mouths. As her eyes drifted closed, her mind turned off to negative thoughts, the world ablaze with vibrations that were brand new in their intensity.

He was carrying her across the room and she knew when he stopped they were next to the bed. She opened her eyes when his lips left hers and found him staring at her, his gaze glimmering with starlight.

She shouldn't have opened her eyes. Meeting his gaze brought back the reality of what she was about to sacrifice. Not her body, for it had proven itself more than willing to lose itself in this man's embrace, to be absorbed and assimilated, protected and cherished.

Not her body, but rather her independence. Her tenuous grip on establishing autonomy. Maybe casual sex could happen with someone for whom she harbored no deep feelings, but that was impossible with this man.

As all this raced through her mind, he lowered his head to kiss the hollow of her throat, to lick her overheated skin. How she wanted to turn off her thoughts. She closed her eyes, once again consumed with everything he did, shuddering as his lips nuzzled her breasts, still covered with satin, the delirious moistness of his mouth just a whisper away and hers for the taking.

He knelt on the mattress, gently laying her atop the plush comforter. Again their eyes met as he slipped his hand under the pajama top and his fingers rubbed her nipples. With his free hand he undid the buttons, and the cloth fell open. He looked at her as though she was a banquet, his desire tripling her own, the groan in his throat reverberating through her body. He trailed kisses across her stomach as his fingers inched beneath the waistband of her bottoms and he murmured her name.

Her name.

"Stop," she said so softly, it might have been the

beat of a butterfly wing. But he heard her, and relief was followed by a stab of regret.

Within a few seconds, he was stretched out beside her, caressing her as he looked into her eyes. "What's wrong, Faith?"

She sat up abruptly, holding her pajama top closed across her sensitive breasts, ashamed she'd allowed things to go this far. "I just can't," she said. "I'm sorry. This is my fault."

He slowly sat up, his thigh touching hers. "I should have known it was too good to be true," he murmured.

"I thought I could."

"I had high hopes, too," he said, smoothing the hair away from her face. He kissed her lips and her eyelids.

"I can't turn off my head," she admitted as she fumbled with her buttons.

"This has to do with what you said last night."

She nodded.

"I guess I don't understand," he told her, sitting expectantly, as though waiting for a better explanation. Which, she figured, she owed him.

"I moved here because of a job, it's true. Because I have medical expenses to pay, debts to clear. But I also moved here because I had to get away from my father and big brother. Both of them are a lot like you, Trip."

"I'm not sure how to take that."

"They're take-control men—*round up the women and children, keep them safe* type of men."

"And that's what you think I am."

"That's what you are."

"And that's so terrible?"

"No, that's admirable. But I'm the kind of woman who wants nothing more than to be taken care of. I don't like being scared. I don't like being alone."

"Then we're a match made in heaven," he said with an attempt at a smile.

"I don't want to be that kind of woman anymore. I know that kind of woman is vulnerable and weak and a victim. She lives in a fool's paradise, a fantasy world."

"How did we go from sex to you leaning on me?"

"Because I care about you. Sex with you, for me, well, it wouldn't be a casual thing, a forget-about-it-tomorrow thing."

He stood abruptly and stared down at her. "Who says it has to be that?"

"I do."

"Because?"

"Because I can't allow myself to need you."

"God, it's a vicious circle with you. I don't honestly think you know what you want."

"And you do know what you want?"

He looked taken aback by her question. She got the feeling he didn't worry about things like this very often. He was a man of action, not a man of endless speculation. He finally said, "Of course I do."

She met his gaze. "You're a former FBI agent," she said. "You came in here tonight talking about Neil Roberts, about how 'we'll' get him, like you still work for the Bureau. Face it, you are who you are, and it's not a rancher. So, why are you pretending?"

He took a step toward her. "Isn't that kind of obvious?"

"Oh, I know you left the FBI and undercover work for honorable reasons, but couldn't you have taken a less dangerous job within the organization and stayed doing what you love?"

"This is a family ranch. I have to preserve it for Noelle and Colin."

"But it's not how you want to spend your life, is it? You haven't even made this place your own."

Now he raised his hands and dropped them. "I don't have the slightest idea what you're talking about."

"You know what I mean. There's no sign of you in the house. It's like you're camping there."

"I am not going to have this discussion with you," he said flatly, eyes blazing.

But she was on a roll, and bigger concerns than Luke Tripper and the Triple T forced the next words out of her mouth. "It can't be good for Colin and Noelle to have you so miserable about living here with them. Wouldn't they be better off with a happy you, in your world, than a sulking you in theirs?"

She'd seen several expressions on his handsome face the past couple of days. Concern, desire, patience and about everything in between, but she hadn't yet witnessed the fury that burned in those dark orbs until now. "Sulk? I do not sulk!"

"Glower, then."

"You're one to talk," he said. "I may have given something up, but at least I didn't run and hide. Talk about sulking."

Hot tears burned behind her eyes as they stared at each other.

"Don't think I don't know why you left half your stuff at that miserable apartment. You want a back door in case you can't face your own feelings."

"How dare you!" she said, but his words had the ring of truth.

He shook his head sadly, and with one last piercing glance, turned his back and left.

BY CONCENTRATING ON RANCH duties, Trip managed to put the episode in the cabin out of his mind until the next morning, when he looked out the kitchen window and saw Faith walking toward the house. His eyes drank in a black coat belted around her trim waist, knee-high boots supple around shapely legs, her limp barely noticeable, her hair floating about her shoulders.

She looked young and beautiful and untouched by the real world. He knew that was an illusion; she wasn't a child, she wasn't an innocent, she was a woman—and she made his blood boil in more ways than one.

He opened the door before she could knock and held up his coffee mug.

"No, thanks, I already had breakfast. I was wondering if you found a car to lend me. I'll rent one later and return yours when I come back tonight to pack my things."

"Ah, the big retreat," he said. "You're good at those."

"Don't start," she warned.

He took a deep breath. "Listen, tempers got the best of us. Maybe something more than tempers. Anyway, we don't have to be best friends to uphold our bargain, do we? I still need help finding a baby-sitter, you still need a place to stay. We'll keep it impersonal." He produced the keys to his sister's vehicle from his pocket and offered them to her.

She stared at the keys for a moment. He could

tell she wanted to tell him what he could do with them, but she was also stuck out in the middle of nowhere with no car. She finally took the keys, closed her hand around them, then looked up at him, obviously searching for the right words.

Noelle burst into the kitchen behind him, making a beeline for Faith. His niece wrapped her arms around Faith and smiled up at her, her backpack slipping off her shoulders.

"Morning sweetie," Faith said, straightening the backpack. Lowering her voice to a whisper, she added, "How's Buster?"

"He's still asleep," Noelle whispered back, as Mrs. Murphy bustled into the kitchen carrying Colin. The moment the baby caught sight of Faith, he kicked his legs and squealed, reaching out to her.

Trip thought of what Faith had said, that he was just going through the motions on this ranch and, by implication, with the children. Was it true?

Colin never drooled all over himself when Trip entered a room. So what did Faith do that he didn't?

Mrs. Murphy tried to contain Colin, but Faith stepped past Trip, Noelle trailing behind, and took the baby into her arms, kissing his cheeks as he grabbed handfuls of her hair. She quickly disengaged his hands and kissed him one last time before handing him back to the housekeeper.

Okay, she kissed Colin a lot, and she hugged and smiled at Noelle, so maybe that was it—maybe he needed to get more physical with the kids. *Talk to them more. Play games. Frolic, for God's sake.*

Gazing up at Faith, Noelle asked, "Can I ride to school with you?"

"Not today," Faith said, brushing Noelle's bangs away from her forehead. "I have an early meeting with Principal Cooper. Tomorrow is the last day of school before Christmas break. How about we go together then?" She glanced briefly at Trip and added, "If it's okay with your uncle."

"Sure," Trip said, wondering if it was safe for Noelle to be alone with Faith in case David Lee tried something. Well, there was no law against Trip tailing her, was there? He was pretty damn good at that, even on deserted roads. Great skill to have as a rancher.

Of course, if she caught him there'd be hell to pay. There was nothing to be done about it but tell her the truth. Tonight.

Noelle nodded vigorously as Faith went back outside.

"It's the red sedan in the second garage," Trip called out.

"Where's the second garage?"

That gave him an excuse to go help her. Maybe a few more sentences would further diffuse the tension between them. "I'll get my coat—" he began, but just then George Plum and Eddie Reed appeared around the corner of the house.

Faith immediately asked them about the location of the second garage and to his surprise, Eddie Reed was the one who responded. "I looked through all the outbuildings when I got here early this morning," he said.

"Then you know where the red car is."

"Sure. Come on, I'll show you. Be right back, Mr. Plum."

As George tapped out his pipe before entering the kitchen, Faith and Eddie walked off toward the second garage. Why was he so disappointed he wasn't the one escorting her? Why couldn't he seem to stay angry with her?

His mind flashed back to those few blissful moments when she'd let down her guard, when he'd felt the ripeness of her body beneath the silky pajamas and then the sight of her beautiful, firm flesh. The taste of her skin, her softness…

And then all the crap that followed.

Behind him, the sounds of morning exploded, as Colin wailed about something, Noelle chattered to Mrs. Murphy and George Plum poked at the fire on the hearth. Trip closed the door. He'd go into the newspaper office after taking Noelle to school, put an ad in the classifieds, see if Sheriff Torrence was hanging around the diner so he could pump him for information about David Lee, then come back home to work on ranch business.

It occurred to him he shouldn't ask about Lee. He'd been told to back off.

Well, screw that.

Chapter Nine

There was a world of difference between work that day and the day before. Faith no longer felt on edge, at least not about roving murderers. She no longer glanced out the window or started every time someone passed the open doorway of her room. The children were so excited about the coming vacation that they were rowdy and wild and she gave up trying to do anything more than just have fun with them. Even Noelle seemed to enter into the spirit.

She watched through her window as Trip picked Noelle up after school. She didn't want to face him again, dreaded another conversation of almost any kind. Hadn't they said quite enough last night?

With time to herself, she parked the red sedan downtown and joined the Christmas shoppers. She'd already sent small gifts home to her family, but now it appeared she'd be at the Tripper house for Christmas. It was fun choosing something for

Noelle and Colin and even Mrs. Murphy. Trip was different. What did a woman buy a man who attracted her and angered her the way this one did?

She didn't have the faintest idea.

She paid extra to have the store wrap the three gifts she did buy. They were very modest presents, but it still took half her available cash. Maybe by next Christmas, she'd be able to see a light at the end of her debtor's tunnel.

She'd just come out of the store and was digging for the car keys in her purse when someone slammed into her. Packages went flying as two hands grabbed her. She looked up into the eyes of David Lee.

In one instant, her mouth went dry. Even the cheery Christmas music piped on to the sidewalk seemed to fade as she tried to tear herself away from his fierce grip.

But he wasn't having any of it. He pinned her in place, eyes narrowed, face flushed with deadly excitement, inches from hers. She looked over his shoulder, hoping another pedestrian would notice her predicament, but the sidewalk was empty. She was on the verge of screaming, in hopes someone inside the store would come to her aid, but no sound could make its way up her throat.

Where was everyone? It was like the earth had suddenly emptied and they were alone.

"You bitch," David said, his voice a thin hiss, his breath sour and hot.

"Let…let go of me," she stammered, finally finding her voice. Once again she struggled to escape, but David was solid as a rock with vise grips for hands.

"Now I got the sheriff breathing down my neck," he continued. "I should have come back and taken care of you when I had the chance."

"Then you admit you ran me off the road," she said.

"I don't admit nothing."

"Let go of me," she repeated.

"Not before you get a little taste of what I'm going to give you next time I find you alone, baby." His lips curled as his head dipped toward hers.

Fear was suddenly replaced by rage. Bracing herself on her left leg, she sharply drew up her right knee and forced it smack dab into David Lee's groin.

He screamed, released his grip, doubled over and clutched himself. In the next instant, another man shouted. That was all Faith noticed as the impact of kneeing David jolted her injured leg and blinded her with pain. She sagged as someone supported her elbows.

She managed to make out Eddie Reed's concerned face. "Do you know that guy?" he said. "I saw him grab you."

She nodded, shaky but oddly proud of herself. Over Eddie's shoulder she could see David's hunched form staggering away down the sidewalk, one shoulder hunkered against the buildings he passed to keep from falling over.

"His name is David Lee. You're about the same age. I'm surprised you didn't go to school with him."

"I went to school in Laxton," Eddie said, gesturing vaguely eastward. "Did he hurt you?"

"Not as bad as I hurt him," she said, and despite everything, smiled.

Looking at his hands wrapped around her sleeves he said, "Are you steady now?"

"Sure, I'm good."

After stuffing a small hardware bag into his coat pocket, Eddie helped Faith pick up her scattered packages. The pungent aroma of lilies suggested Mrs. Murphy's cologne was history.

"Thanks," Faith said, testing her leg. It throbbed, but at least it supported her weight.

"You didn't need my help," Eddie said. "You aren't as dainty as you look."

She put Mrs. Murphy's present in the outside trash can. "Thanks for helping out, I appreciate it."

"No problem. I'll give you a ride back to the ranch. You live out there next to Mr. Tripper, right?"

"Yes. I don't need a ride, though."

"I don't mind…it's no trouble."

"I have a car, remember?" she said, nodding toward the red sedan a spot or two away. For the first time, she noticed it seemed to be sitting a little funny, as though she'd parked it on an incline.

"Oh, yeah, I forgot," Eddie replied.

The reason the car looked funny was that it was tilted. And the reason it was tilted was because all four tires were flat.

"Oh, man, look what that jerk did," Faith said, her heart dropping as she calculated the cost of towing the car and repairing four flats. She twirled around to see how far David Lee had stumbled, ready to somehow force him to pay for it, but he'd disappeared from sight.

"Don't worry, my ride is in front of the hardware store," Eddie said. "I'll come back and fix your tires after I take you home."

Faith wasn't sure how to proceed. At that moment, a truck pulled up in the loading zone. It came as little surprise when Trip rolled down his window. Faith couldn't figure out why she'd expected him, but she had.

He looked from the car, so obviously askew, to Faith to Eddie and back again. "Faith, come with me," he said.

"No, thanks," she said, hoping she sounded breezy. "Eddie is going to help me."

"Please," Trip said, and something in the tone of his voice caught Faith's full attention. She looked at him carefully for the first time. Something was wrong.

"Thanks anyway, Eddie," she said as she unlocked the red sedan and retrieved her book bag. She heard Eddie assure Trip he'd get the garage to look at the tires right away. As Faith slid into the truck beside Trip, he pulled out into the traffic.

"What happened to the car?"

She fastened her seat belt and said, "David Lee. He accosted me on the sidewalk and apparently slashed the tires or let the air out of them or something."

"Accosted you?" he growled, followed by a swift glance. "Did you call the police?"

"Not yet."

"At the risk of getting my head bitten off, I think you should file a complaint. The man is harassing you. You need a restraining order, but that means filling out the forms and presenting them to the court and getting a hearing date. All that takes time. Did Eddie witness the incident?"

"I think so. He tried to come to my rescue." She was silent for a second and then added, "Isn't that odd? Eddie just happened to be around when I needed help, and then you just happened to show up."

"I didn't just happen to show up, I've been looking all over town for you. Besides, Eddie works for George Plum."

"Which is the same as working for you."

"True." He pulled up in front of the police station. "You have to report this to Chief Novak. It wouldn't hurt for the sheriff to know about it, too."

"Honestly, Trip, what did I do before I had you to organize my life?"

"Heaven knows," he said. "Aren't you curious why I came looking for you?"

"I know why you came," she said. "You were worried about David Lee. Well, you were absolutely right to be worried about him, the man is a lowlife." Her throbbing left leg lent passion to her words.

"You told me to back off. You told me you don't want me worrying about you."

"Yeah, well, you don't always listen to what I say, do you?" she asked sweetly.

"In all fairness, I'm not sure you always *mean* what you say," he responded. "Anyway, today you're wrong. It turns out the sighting of Neil Roberts down in San Diego was bogus, a lookalike, nothing more. Some poor guy got bombarded by a SWAT team. Anyway, Roberts is still missing and now the agent I told you about who had a lead on Gene Edwards hasn't been heard of in twenty-four hours."

"And Gene Edwards is who, exactly?"

"The man who helped Neil Roberts kill his third victim and abduct his fourth. The missing agent worked in Idaho. I don't have to remind you how close we are to Idaho, do I?"

"No," Faith said with a shudder.

He put a hand atop hers. "Last night was a mistake," he said softly. "Both of us got things wrong. But this is bigger than you needing space and me figuring out how to be a father and us dealing with our feelings for each other. This is life and death. Don't fight me on this."

She looked at his fingers lying across hers. He was right, of course. It was time to stop being afraid and angry and for them to work together to make sure Colin and Noelle stayed safe. "Okay. We'll do it your way."

THE POLICE STATION LOOKED very much the same as it had the only other time Trip had been inside. Lenny was at the desk, shuffling a stack of papers. When he got a good look at Faith, he straightened his shoulders and came to life. "Can I help you?" he asked, drinking in Faith as though she was a cold bottle of water in the middle of a 10K marathon.

"I need to fill out a complaint," Faith said.

"Sure, oh, yeah, I got forms," Lenny said, mumbling his words in his anxiety to please her.

"While the lady does that, I want to see Duke Perry, my former mechanic. Is he still here?"

"Yeah. I'll take you in. Be right back, Miss. Uh, don't leave."

They walked past the chief's closed door. Trip could hear voices coming from inside and hoped his luck held to the point where he got in and out of the station without actually facing Novak.

The cell block was a simple, old-fashioned situation not seen around much anymore. Three cells, two of them empty, Duke sitting on a cot in the last one. Trip didn't know if he should credit his FBI years, or the fact that a beautiful young woman waited back in the front, but Lenny quickly left him there alone, with directions to buzz the bell by the door when he was ready to leave.

Duke was in his late thirties, long brown hair worn in a ponytail, tattoos up and down his arms. He had a scraggly beard that hung to midchest, a soft voice and red-rimmed eyes that currently had a hard time meeting Trip's.

Trip pulled a chair up to the bars. "Duke, I just wanted to tell you I'm sorry you let this happen."

"Me, too," Duke said.

"I guess I want to know how it came about. I want to make sure you deserve to be here. You were doing so good."

Duke looked at Trip and then away. He got off

the cot and walked to the far corner where he found himself the shelter of a shadow. "I don't know," he said.

"I don't buy that. You told me you never even went to the tavern anymore, that you'd decided to stay away from temptation."

"Listen," Duke said. "I could blame it on the nice guy buying me rounds of drinks, I could blame it on the cold night or the fact my woman took up with her boss last month. What difference does it make?"

"None," Trip admitted. "I just wish you hadn't gotten behind a wheel."

"Yeah, well, me, too. Hindsight and all that. Tell you the truth, I'm glad someone called me in, glad I didn't hurt no one."

"Absolutely. I'll get George Plum to cut you a check for what we owe you."

"I appreciate that. Maybe I can make bail, go stay with my brother for a while."

Trip put the chair back where it belonged and buzzed his way out. Faith was waiting for him, papers filled out, ready to leave as soon as Lenny finished telling her what she should do next. Trip looked up as he heard a door open, and then grimaced to himself. He'd stayed too long. Novak and another man were coming out of the chief's office.

Novak towered over a much younger, smaller man, a guy with shaggy brown hair and a dark gaze that slid over both Trip and Faith. Besides the scowl on his face, he wore scruffy blue jeans and a flannel shirt, a padded denim jacket tucked under one arm.

"You stay in town, you hear?" Novak snarled.

"You got nothing against me," the man said, flinging up the section of the counter that was hinged to allow passage and letting it bang down in his wake, brushing close to Faith in his haste. "I'm as worried about Gina as anyone else," he shouted. "I don't know where she is."

"Gina?" Trip said, staring hard at the man. "Are you Peter Saks?"

"What's it to you?" he snapped.

"My name is Luke Tripper. I'm Gina's boss."

The man Trip assumed was Peter Saks seemed to swell in size as he threw a punch at Trip's face. Trip caught his fist midair and twisted his arm behind his back. Leaning over the smaller man's shoulder, Trip said, "What's your problem, buddy?"

"Let go of me."

"Not if you're going to start a fight," Trip said. He looked around to see Faith backed up against a wall, Lenny gawking and Chief Novak grinning.

"I won't start nothin'," the man grumbled as

some of the fight seemed to drain from his body. Trip released him. The man took a few steps, rubbing his hand on his jeans. "Yeah, I'm Peter Saks," he added, "and this is all your fault."

Trip leaned over, snagged the fallen jacket from the floor and tossed it at Saks. "What's my fault?"

Saks caught the jacket and shrugged it on. "Gina breaking up with me and then running away. What did you say to her?"

"You've lost me," Trip said.

"She had the hots for you. She was going to tell you. Did you make fun of her?"

Trip was pretty sure he would have known if Gina was truly infatuated with him—but maybe not. He hadn't given her a second thought beyond her responsibilities as the babysitter, so he supposed she might have indulged in a fantasy or two. But he sure as hell knew she'd never said anything to him about it. That he would remember. "I thought the consensus around here is she went camping with you."

"Not with me. She wouldn't give me the time of day. I barely got to California before my dad called and told me everyone thought Gina was with me. So I came back here to clear things up and to tell the cops they should be looking at you, not me."

Running a hand through his hair, Trip said, "Gina never said a word to me. And even if she did harbor…well…feelings for me, why would she abandon her car like that? It doesn't make sense."

Novak finally spoke up. "And that's why Mr. Saks is going to stay here in town while I look into this more closely."

Novak had already wasted two days, and worse, as far as Trip was concerned, so had he. He'd gotten so tied up with Faith and his concerns about Neil Roberts and David Lee that he'd let Gina's disappearance fall by the wayside.

"Gina was my girl before you came to Shay," Peter Saks fumed.

Trip lowered his voice and stared right into Saks's eyes. "I know you hit her before. She told me."

Saks's fists balled at his sides, but he apparently thought better of expressing his outrage. He turned abruptly and pushed his way through the door.

"See there, Lenny," Novak said with a chuckle as the door slammed behind Saks, "that there is how the FBI handles a suspect. Thanks for the lesson, Trip."

Trip swallowed an oath and said nothing.

Lenny smiled. "That guy was mad, all right."

"He's a hothead," Novak said.

While Trip agreed with this assessment, it was impossible not to speculate if that's all he was. One fact was undeniable: Gina was gone and no one seemed to know where she was.

"Something I can do for you folks?" Novak added.

"Miss Bishop here said David Lee pushed her around on the sidewalk today," Lenny said.

"Another hothead," Novak muttered. "Harmless, though."

"And Mr. Tripper wanted to see Duke Perry."

"You siding with a drunk?" the chief asked, narrowing his eyes.

"Of course not."

"That's smart. We got a Good Samaritan call about him leaving the tavern, weaving down the sidewalk, getting in his damn car. Blew point ten, couldn't walk a straight line—we got him dead to rights so you can just—"

"Go back to my ranch, I know," Trip finished. Taking Faith's hand, he added, "Let's get out of here."

"Is there something in the water around here?" Faith asked as they once again rattled over the cattle guard and came to a stop on the other side. Faith turned to witness a man get out of a truck parked beside the fence. The man proceeded to close a gate Faith had never been aware of before. He carried a rifle with practiced ease.

"What do you mean?"

The clang of steel banging against steel sent a reassuring surge through Faith. The man waved them off. Turning to face forward again, she said,

"David Lee, Peter Saks—they're about the same age and they're both spooky."

"Isn't the new guy about the same age, too, and he seems calm enough."

"Eddie what's-his-name…Reed. Yeah. Wait, he didn't grow up in Shay. Maybe it's the school system and not the water."

"That's why we need good teachers like you," Trip said as he parked between the house and Faith's cabin. There was no sign of the red sedan. "Before you go," he added, "I don't think it's a good idea for Noelle to leave the ranch tomorrow."

She looked at him closely. "Because of Neil Roberts?"

"Yes. Frankly, I wish you'd call in sick, too, but I know better than to try to stop you."

"It's the last day of school before break."

"I know. Will you at least let me or someone else drive you? I'll have the sedan delivered to the school by the time you're ready to come home."

As she'd all but destroyed her car two days ago and been indirectly responsible for the tire incident with the sedan, she didn't figure she had much ground to stand on when it came to protest. Anyway, now that his demands had become requests, she was finding it easier to go along with him. "Okay, that's fine. Thank you."

"I put an ad in the paper, to start running

Saturday," he told her as they got out of the truck. "There's an existing phone line into the cabin, so you can get calls there or in the house. That way, you can organize interviews. But I want to ask you to schedule them all for later next week. Let's give this mess with Roberts a few more days before we start inviting strangers out here."

"Whatever you say." He looked surprised by her cooperation. "I'm not an idiot," she added.

"I never thought you were. Do you know how to handle a gun? Because if you do, I'll see to it you're armed, at least while you're here on the ranch."

"I never learned about guns. It never seemed important to know how to handle one. My brother tried to get me to learn, but I was too stubborn."

Was that a smile he turned away to hide? They got out of the truck, and at the point where Faith should veer off to head to the cabin, she caught Trip's arm. "I'd like to see the kids. If it's okay with you."

"Sure." He waited until she'd preceded him into the front hall to add, "Would you like to stay and eat supper with us?"

She knew she shouldn't because she knew she wanted to. But she also admitted to herself she didn't want to go sit in the cabin with a belly full of fear, waiting for something to happen when darkness descended.

But those weren't the only reasons, and she admitted that, too. She craved Trip's companionship as well as time with the children, and that was a fact. She was a family girl, a homebody, a people person trying to be a loner. It was tricky to go against nature, hence all the advances and retreats.

As Noelle ran down the stairs, Faith mumbled, "Actually, I'd like to stay," and felt like a dismal failure.

A FEW HOURS LATER, she rocked Colin to sleep, his baby warmth so at odds with the internal cold she couldn't shake. For a long while she stood over his crib, studying his face in repose, trying to see him as his mother must have seen him, must have thought she'd always see him. There was a picture of her on the wall nearby, and it almost looked as though her gaze were focused on the crib. As this wasn't Colin's nursery at the time of Susan's death, it meant someone else had put the picture there after she died.

A terrible sadness swelled in Faith's heart, both for Trip's sister and for the children she left behind. How cruel and arbitrary life could be.

But at least Colin had his uncle, and Faith smiled as she touched the baby's spiky, reddish-blond hair. She'd been amused when Trip rescued Colin from his high chair during dinner and suffered bits of mashed potatoes and strained carrots flung every which way. When he'd caught her eye and smiled, she felt a giant lump in her throat.

She finally returned to the living room and found Trip cuddling Noelle on his lap. He was reading to her, the huge decorated Christmas tree a backdrop. Trip was assuming voices as he read, which made Noelle relax back against his chest where she giggled.

In a couple of weeks, Faith would move away from here and these people would continue their lives without her. Trip would run the ranch, maybe even growing to appreciate it as the years went by. The children would flourish, the three of them would continue to knit themselves into a family. And one day Trip would meet a woman who fit their lives. He would marry her and they would all live happily ever after.

The story ended, Noelle all but asleep. Trip's cell phone rang, jarring the child from her stupor. As he took the call, Faith led Noelle upstairs. The taut nerves of earlier had mellowed as the evening progressed without incident, but they came back as she recalled the wary look in Trip's eyes as he walked into the den. She'd heard the curt tone of his voice and the silence with which he listened to his caller.

Now what?

Noelle pulled Faith from her distressing thoughts when she uttered in a drowsy voice, "I don't want to miss school tomorrow. Alicia is bringing cupcakes."

Faith tucked Buster in beside her. "I'll save one for you," she whispered.

For a few minutes, she sat by Noelle's bed, holding her hand until the little girl's fingers slipped from her grip. With a final kiss to the child's forehead, she half closed the door against the slanted light from the hall. She found Trip in his small bedroom, standing at the window, sliding home the lock. "That's the last one," he said, turning, but one look at her face and he added, "You okay?"

"I'm a little on edge. I told you I was a giant coward."

"Only fools don't have nerves," he said gently. "Or maybe the innocent. Like the children. I hope they didn't sense the tension."

"I think Noelle was too busy enjoying you reading to her."

"I'm not very good at it."

"You sell yourself short. I thought your aardvark voice was brilliant."

He smiled, and then his expression grew serious. "I know you're curious about the phone call," he began as he approached her.

"I'm almost afraid to ask."

He stopped beside her in the doorway. He was standing too close. There was no reason for such intimacy except for the most basic reason of all. Despite their heated accusations, there was something between them and had been from the beginning. That something made personal boundaries obsolete. Somehow, within the last twenty-four hours, they'd moved forward with each other, though Faith wasn't sure how it had happened.

"Colby called," he said, leaning toward her, bracing himself with a hand on the doorjamb above her head. It took her a second to remember that Colby was his old boss at the FBI. Her heart skidded to a stop. "They found the missing agent," he added, "the man I told you had a lead on Gene Edwards. He's dead, shot through the heart."

"Oh, no! I'm so sorry."

"He was a family man. Left a wife and a little girl. Damn it to hell."

Not that many hours ago, she'd chastised him for not staying in the FBI once he became guardian to Colin and Noelle, and now an agent was dead. How could she have been such a know-it-all?

"Faith, maybe you should leave."

"No," she said.

"I don't want something happening to you or the children."

"What about you?"

"No, I have to stop him. If he's coming here, I have to stop him once and for all."

"But there are others who can do that."

"No." He said it in such a way that she knew the subject was closed.

"We're safer near you than away from you, Trip. Besides, they may not be coming at all."

"Maybe."

He needed comforting and so did she. As she put her arms around his solid torso, the warmth of his body seeped into hers. A hard bulge under his suede vest reminded her he wore a gun in a shoulder strap, that he took the threat against the house and the people inside it very seriously. "I'm sorry about the agent," she said as his arms circled her. He held her so close it was hard to breathe. That was okay, she needed his closeness way more than she needed oxygen.

"Every law enforcement agent knows this is a possibility," he said.

"His poor wife."

"Yes."

She looked up at him. His mouth was very close, his face crisscrossed with shadows. She took a deep breath as she peered into his dark eyes and said, "Someday you'll fall in love."

He ran a finger along the small scar and across her lips. "Do you think so?"

"Yes, of course you will."

"Will she be a blonde with big blue eyes?"

"She'll be brave," Faith said. "She'll be fear-less."

"She sounds rather formidable."

"She'll know what she wants. Who she wants."

"And that someone will be me?"

"Yes."

"Lucky me," he whispered. His lips brushed her forehead, then her ear, and he added, "I know I'm going to regret this," and in the next moment his lips touched hers.

The house might be very quiet, but the thunder-ing in Faith's head sounded like a herd of wild horses unleashed. His mouth was incredibly soft, welcoming, a homecoming for her soul. He gathered her around the waist and held on to her as though she might slip through his grasp, and she dug her fingernails into his shoulders to keep from spinning to the ground. He whispered against her ear, "Tell me right now to get my hands off you."

"I—"

"Because if you don't, there's no stopping. Not tonight, not ever again. This is fair warning. Think about what you want. Last night you were so sure."

This was closeness, this was merging, this was needing and being needed. It didn't mean she was backing away from her goals, it just meant that she wasn't being rigid.

That was her story and she was sticking with it.

"Ssh," she said as she claimed his mouth.

Chapter Ten

The trip from the upstairs of the house to the cabin happened in a daze. Trip left her side but once, and that was to talk to a guard he'd posted in the kitchen.

Once in the cabin, they turned on no lights, but the moon had broken through the cloud cover and streamed in the skylight, bathing the cabin in shimmering silver.

With the door locked behind them, they once again fell into each other's arms. She was glad he wasn't asking her to explain her change of heart when it came to making love—she really had no sensible explanation except that she knew she had to have him, even if it was just once. Anyway, what did good sense have to do with emotions as vibrant as those she felt when Trip took her in his arms?

He gently pushed her onto the bed in a sitting position and knelt before her, unlacing her shoes, slipping them from her feet. Next came her socks, and then he pulled her upright. As she stood in the moonlight, he unzipped her trousers and pulled them down her legs, steadying her as she stepped out of them. She could feel the suppressed energy in his hands as he unbuttoned her blouse and released the front closure on her bra, freeing her breasts. She stood naked before him, and she watched as his gaze caressed her like loving hands. When his gaze lingered for a moment on the scars across her abdomen, she started to cover herself. He caught her hands.

"Don't hide," he whispered.

"But the scars—"

"Are part of you. They're nothing to worry about."

She had to see him naked, too. Stepping closer, she slipped his vest off his broad shoulders and added it to the growing pile of clothes on the floor. He unbuckled the shoulder holster and took it off, laying the gun aside, and then she slowly undid his shirt buttons, pausing when she got to his waist, where she unbuckled his belt and unbuttoned his jeans. He helped her by taking off his shirt and then she pulled his jeans down his long legs and then his underwear until he stepped free of his clothes and stood before her cast in pewter, as perfect as a man could be, the visible signs of his excitement making Faith quiver inside.

She touched him as his fingers caressed her breasts, ran down her stomach, slipped between her legs. In the next instant, their bodies pressed together in a desperate attempt to get as close as possible, until he lifted her from her feet and she wrapped her legs around him. They tumbled onto the bed, penetration coming as long, deep thrusts with no more preamble. She dug her fingers into the solid mounds of his buttocks, head back, eyes closed, until his mouth once again found hers and his tongue plunged the same way his pelvis did. The world shrank in on itself, reduced to two people and the passion that burned the silver night until their groans of fulfillment merged into one.

She had no idea sex could be this way. That it could consume like a forest fire, and yet leave a person feeling renewed and not damaged, that need could rise and fall like a frantic pulse until a deep peace fell, an all-consuming lethargy.

Sometime later, he kissed her awake. "I have to go," he said softly as her eyelashes fluttered open. She reached for him as he sat up.

"Where are you going?"

He leaned over and gently kissed her lips. "Back inside."

Of course.

"I don't want to," he added. He kissed her again and then got off the bed. She watched him dress, the sight of him in the moonlight arousing every sense. The bed felt lonely without him.

He murmured good night as he slipped out the door. The lock sprang closed behind him.

TRIP SAT IN THE TRUCK for a moment, watching Faith walk into the school, reluctant to leave until the doors closed behind her.

It wasn't just that watching her was such a fine way to spend a few moments, although there was always that. He blinked a few times to purge the memory of her naked body from his mind, knowing if he let it dwell there he'd be happy to sit like a moron for hours.

Oh, the sweet, sweet softness of her. The smoothness, the roundness. The sounds she made, the way she held on to him, the feelings she stirred so deep in his body that it surely had to touch his soul. A man could become addicted to a woman like Faith. Hopelessly addicted.

She looked over her shoulder at the door and the flash of a smile touched her lips, then she disappeared. He grinned to himself like some lusty schoolboy, already planning the next time they'd meet, the next time they'd be alone.

For some unexplainable reason, he flashed back to the bus disaster, to the woman he hadn't been able to save. For the first time since it happened, he felt a sense of peace about it. The regret and sorrow would always be there, yes, but now he knew he could put it in perspective. And he knew he had Faith to thank.

He finally headed over to Shay's Diner. He'd seen the sheriff's car in the lot on his way into town and hoped to catch him before he left. He was relieved to find the cruiser still in the parking lot.

Trip entered the diner, taking off his hat, greeting a table of ranchers who had been friends of his father's. All of them were over sixty now, hard-bitten men with rangy bodies and weathered skin, meeting to talk about feed and livestock and market prices. He knew he would be welcome to join them by simple virtue of his father's reputation, but he wasn't really one of them. He thought he'd probably never be one of them, not in any valid way.

He was an imposter, and he knew they knew it.

He looked around for Marnie, but she must have been picking up an order in the back, as she wasn't working the coffee carafe as usual. The sheriff had a booth to himself. Trip slid in across from him and the two men greeted each other.

"You want to know what I'm doing about David Lee," the sheriff said, as he shoveled in a forkful of hash browns.

"You're a mind reader." Trip turned his coffee cup over and looked around for someone to fill it.

"We found paint on Miss Bishop's car and one

tire track up near where she went off that we can't trace to her vehicle or yours. The state lab has everything we've collected." He took a long swallow of coffee. "When we get a definitive lead on the color and tire size of the vehicle we're looking for, we'll start in on David Lee's buddies. I got a deputy trying to break alibis right now. Hell, you know the drill."

A waitress Trip had seen a couple of times before sidled up to the table. "What'll you have?" she said while filling Trip's mug.

"Just coffee, thanks." She was off in a flash. The place was packed and seemed short-staffed. Trip watched Torrence dip his toast into his egg yolk before adding, "Lee threatened Faith last night."

"So she told me. Did she file a complaint with Chief Novak? Is she going after a restraining order?"

"That depends on Lee's next move. Novak said he'd talk to the guy." He didn't add that he thought another conversation with Lee was a waste of time.

"I'll call the lab today and see if they have anything, try to hurry them up."

"Thanks. And then there's the matter of my babysitter. Novak is sure Gina's boyfriend has something to do with it, but the boyfriend says he's innocent, and for some reason I believe him."

"You're talking about Peter Saks?"

"Yeah."

"Another troublemaker. He was in the diner yesterday morning, throwing his weight around, giving everyone grief."

"I don't get why Gina's mother and the chief are so complacent about the fact she left and hasn't checked in. I've been calling the mother every day and she can barely drum up the enthusiasm to talk to me."

"I heard the girl has a history of running off."

"Still…"

Just then, a raised voice boomed through the diner. It seemed to come from the direction of the kitchen. A man burst through the double doors, looked around the room and zeroed in on Sheriff Torrence.

In a flash, the man was out from behind the counter and threading his way through the restaurant. He stopped in front of Torrence and said, "What are you doing about it? What is anyone doing about it? My God, how long has she been gone?"

Trip stood up. The newcomer looked like he was in his late thirties, tall, athletic build, dark blond hair and a prominent Adam's apple. He was dressed in a crumpled gray suit and he'd pulled the knot on his pale blue tie away from his neck.

"Sit down," Trip said firmly.

The man looked at Trip as though he'd suggested flying to the stars, but he slid in next to Torrence and folded his hands in front of him as though to keep them from pounding on something. "What are you doing to find her?"

How was this guy related to Gina? Maybe a father or an uncle. Maybe Gina's mother was finally getting concerned. He felt a tremendous wave of relief flood his nervous system. Finally someone was taking the disappearance of the girl seriously.

"Why don't you start by telling me your name?" Torrence said, as he pushed his half-eaten meal away. "And who are you talking about?"

"My wife, for God's sake. Don't tell me no one knows she's gone."

Gina, married?

"And your wife is—"

"Marnie Pincer. I'm Nate Pincer."

Trip's relief washed away as quickly as it had arrived. He looked closely at Nate Pincer, trying to remember his and Marnie's courtship. It was a blur; he'd been getting ready for college, hadn't been to the wedding.

What had Marnie mentioned about her husband? He traveled a lot on business. That's right, he represented a line of high-end office furniture.

"When's the last time you saw your wife, Mr. Pincer?" Trip asked.

Pincer was too upset to question Trip's authority to ask questions. "Two days ago. No, three. I left after work that day to drive up to Seattle. I had appointments up there. I was supposed to come home last night, but I think I got a mild case of food poisoning from the crab salad I ate for lunch." He exhaled heavily. "Anyway, I couldn't keep driving so I checked into a motel and tried to call Marnie to tell her I wouldn't be home, but she didn't answer our phone. The damn woman refuses to get a cell phone."

"Did you find it unusual she didn't answer?" the sheriff asked.

"No, Marnie has lots of friends—she often goes to a movie with one of them or gets together to play cards. I planned on calling her back later, but I fell asleep. Woke up this morning and drove straight into town, dropped my bag off at the house and came over here to see her."

"Did your house look normal?"

"What do you mean?"

"Did it look as though there had been trouble there? Broken windows, that kind of thing."

"No, no, nothing."

"What about her car, Nate?" Trip asked. "Was it at your house?"

"Yeah."

"Didn't you think that was odd?"

"I figured she caught a ride with Doris or one of the other gals. She does that sometimes."

"And you asked in the kitchen if anyone had seen her today?" Trip asked.

"Yeah. They said she went home yesterday right after the breakfast service because she didn't feel good. Maybe it wasn't the crab salad that made me sick, maybe she and I had a virus or something and it hit us on the same day."

"You and Marnie getting along?" Torrence asked, his voice casual.

"Yes. What a question!" Nate snarled. Had there been a slight hesitation before he spoke?

"I suppose you called her friends?" Trip said.

"Not yet. I was so sure she'd be here. She was on today's schedule, she never misses work. Never."

Torrence put his napkin on his plate. "Let me out of here. I'll go ask some questions." Nate slid off the bench seat and Torrence got up. He made his way to the kitchen with his characteristic self-assured stride.

Nate shook his head as he seemed to collapse onto the seat.

"Did you call the hospital?" Trip said.

"This is a small town," Nate answered. "Marnie knows everyone. If she was at a friend's house or sick, someone would have notified me. Why didn't she call? She expected me home last night. If someone gave her a ride somewhere, why don't they call me?"

All good questions. Trip had years of practice masking his emotions, so it was with calm detachment he said, "Torrence will find her."

Nate looked hopeful. "Do you really believe that?"

"Sure," Trip said.

"You think she's just at a friend's house or something?"

"That's the way these things usually work out," Trip explained, but the truth was he felt uneasy. There were two women missing now, and experience warned him their disappearances were connected in some way. On the other hand, Gina might have met some new guy and gone off on a lark, and Marnie Pincer could have had a fight with her husband and be cooling off somewhere. She was a grown woman, and nobody even knew how long she'd been gone.

FAITH WRAPPED UP HER day at the grammar school to find the keys to the red sedan, its tires properly inflated, waiting for her in the office. Once inside the car, she discovered a piece of paper taped to the steering column. Unfolded, it revealed a red heart, and written within the heart it said simply, "Sorry I can't meet you. Please go straight home before it gets dark. New developments." It was signed with a *T.*

She smiled despite the portentous feel of the words *new developments,* and even ran a fingertip over the lines. The heart was hand-drawn and wasn't much more refined than those her students produced, but it was a work of art to Faith, and she tucked it away for safekeeping.

New developments. That was a wide open field if ever she heard one. First thing that came to mind was something to do with David Lee, but there were other names that followed. Neil Roberts, Gene Edwards, Gina Cooke, even the dead agent in Idaho whose name she couldn't recall. Her gaze strayed repeatedly to the rearview mirror as she drove home.

Home. Deceptive word. A word with connotations that didn't really fit her situation. But for now she let the word and all its meanings wrap her like a warm blanket. She was going home to see Trip, and that's all she really cared about at the moment. She'd figure out the rest later.

Much later.

There was a different armed guard at the Triple T gate, and as he moved to help her, she gazed down the long line of fencing in an attempt to see if the entire place was surrounded. It had to be, didn't it? Wouldn't the cows wander off if it wasn't? She'd heard the ranch hands talking about mending fences and moving cattle and using the tractor to get feed to different pastures, but it was all so foreign. Peering now into the waning daylight, she could make out dark brown shapes near the top of a rolling hill. Part of the herd, no doubt, maybe the very cows she'd heard lowing as she lay awake last night once Trip left her bed.

Just how big a ranch was the Triple T? How much land, how many head of cattle? She knew they used horses to work the ranch during the summer, but she hadn't gotten down to the barn that housed them yet. There hadn't been time to find out any of the details, and she thought ahead to the next two weeks and what she might learn.

She drove up to the house to find Mrs. Murphy standing at the kitchen door with a bubbly looking Colin attached to her hip. The housekeeper looked anything but bubbly.

"Is Trip here?" Faith asked as she approached, and as usual, the baby reacted to her by kicking and squealing and reaching for her. The little guy was a real ego booster, for sure, and she took him from Mrs. Murphy, kissing his cheeks and nuzzling his sweet neck.

"No, he called a while ago, said he was caught

up in some doings in town. If you can watch the wee one, I'll walk down the to the machine shop and get Noelle." Her lips thinned. "She's been following George Plum around today. I swear that man spoils her rotten."

"Why don't I put a jacket on Colin and we'll walk down there for you," Faith offered. "Maybe you could put your feet up for a bit."

"That would be heaven—I'll make myself a pot of tea. Thank you, lass."

Mrs. Murphy insisted on putting Colin in enough layers for a trek through the Antarctic, while Faith ran to the cabin and changed into jeans and sturdy shoes. She found a baby backpack in the laundry area of the ranch house and tucked Colin into it. The two of them took off with detailed directions for finding the barn that housed the tractors and other ranch equipment. It was the farthest one out, in an area nearest the ranch house.

To get to it, she walked first through the horse barn, where she found Buttercup had been let out of her stall and into an indoor paddock. Colin squealed with delight as the horse trotted up to them and snorted, her breath condensing in the cold air. Faith made a mental note to bring a carrot next time. She patted Buttercup's warm neck as Colin waved his hands and made high-pitched noises. The horse didn't seem to mind the commotion.

Next, they walked through the new construction, which meant she walked the ground where Colin's parents had died. The baby was oblivious, happily playing with Faith's hair and lurching this way and that, but Faith was glad to leave it behind.

By the time they reached the last barn her leg ached. It didn't matter. Kicking David Lee had been good for her soul. The backpack was also hard to handle, digging into her backside and putting strain on bones injured months before. *Note to self: find a stroller.*

The barn appeared to be the oldest structure around, slightly tilted, like a cypress tree on the coast, buffeted by prevailing winds until it listed in the opposite direction. It was dark and cavernous inside, seemingly empty of anything save tractors and trucks and mysterious-looking equipment. She finally heard voices near the back and made her way toward them.

Two men were half-inside the open front hood of a very old truck, their voices alternating as they talked. Faith recognized George Plum's green coat, though neither man looked up or gave any indication they noticed Faith's arrival.

Eddie Reed sat on a stool next to a tractor, a huge box of tools at his feet, work lights trained on the engine in front of him. Noelle sat on a stool next to him, almost buried in a bright red coat and matching knit cap. She was playing with something Faith didn't recognize, talking to herself, off in her own world.

Noelle apparently heard Colin's squeal of excitement upon spying his sister. She looked up suddenly, grinned and jumped off the stool, running to Faith.

"Did you bring me a cupcake?" she asked, staring up at Faith with wide brown eyes so much like her uncle's.

"Of course I brought you a cupcake." She smiled a greeting at Eddie who had looked up from his work, a wrench in his hand. Touching the toy Noelle held, she added, "What's this?"

"Eddie gave it to me," Noelle said, offering it to Faith. "Isn't she so cute? I named her Betsy. Eddie's mommy made it."

Eddie dropped a wrench into the box and stood, wincing as he straightened up. "Been sitting there too long, kind of froze up. Hope it's okay… My mom makes little dolls and I brought one for Noelle."

"I'm sure it's fine," Faith said, admiring the little cloth doll with the embroidered face and hand-sewn dress. Yellow yarn made up the hair. She had a feeling Buster was about to get kicked out of favorite-toy status. "She's adorable. Your mother is talented, Eddie. Do you get to see her often?"

"I live with her," he said.

"Oh, I didn't know that."

"We've always been close," he said. "She's my best friend."

"I hope I get to meet her someday," Faith said.

"Well, she's disabled, you know, can't get out much. But you'd like her. She's a good person."

Faith glanced into Eddie's eyes. There was a kind of lost look in their pale depths with which she could identify. "I've always been very close to my brother and father, too."

"I never knew my real father, and my stepfather walked out on Mama a long time ago," Eddie said. "Left her a Christmas tree farm. It's kind of gone to pot now, though. Mama was never strong enough to do the work. And I don't have time to farm, I got to make us a living."

"Your mother is lucky to have you," Faith said.

"Yeah, well, when I told her about the kids, she insisted I bring them each a toy. Everything she makes is kind of delicate, though. I think the baby is too young for something like that, don't you?"

"Yes, I do. He'd stuff it in his mouth."

Eddie grinned. "Yeah, that's what I told her."

Noelle had wandered off and was standing by George. Faith witnessed the man drop a red and white candy into Noelle's hand. She waited until Noelle had unwrapped it and popped it into her mouth before saying, "Noelle? Mrs. Murphy was looking for you. She says it's time to come back to the house. It'll be dark soon."

Both men looked up from the engine as though just realizing Faith was in the barn. Faith detected the bulge of a handgun under George's long coat. The other man looked away. It was Paul Avery, the "guard" Trip had sent to the school. As always, he seemed nervous around Faith.

"I don't want to go," Noelle garbled around the lump of sugar in her mouth.

"Go on with Ms. Bishop now, before Mrs. Murphy comes looking for you," George said, rubbing his belly. "Damn heartburn," he added.

"Are you sick?" Faith asked. Truth was, George looked kind of sallow.

"No, it's just heartburn." He thumped Avery's arm. "Escort Miss Bishop and the kids back up to the house."

"Yes, sir," Paul said, looking as though he'd rather go skydiving without a parachute. He retrieved a rifle from where he'd propped it against a stack of boxes.

"That's not necessary," Faith protested.

"It's getting dark," George said ominously, with a confirming nod at Paul.

"The boss told us about that killer," Eddie said. "Mean-looking sucker. Better safe than sorry, Miss Bishop, the boss was clear about that."

Paul Avery stayed several steps ahead as they wound their way back through the gloomy barn toward the darkening skies outside.

Chapter Eleven

Trip knocked on Faith's door early the next morning, then used his key to enter.

He found her where he'd left her at midnight, asleep in a tangle of sheets, though she opened one eye as he crossed the floor. He sat down on the mattress next to her, holding a steaming mug of coffee. Her other eye opened.

"Do I have a treat for you," he said.

She sat up, seemingly oblivious for a moment that she was naked, her breasts so inviting he reached for her with his free hand.

Laughing, she pulled up the sheet. "You, sir, have a one-track mind," she said.

"Is that a problem?" he asked, letting his eyes do the wandering.

"No," she murmured.

He handed her the mug. "Two sugars, a drop of cream."

She took a sip and sighed. "Perfect. What's my treat?"

"Remember how last night you were asking questions about the ranch?"

"Blame it on my insatiable thirst for knowledge," she said, nodding. "I now know you raise antibiotic-free cattle, anywhere from five hundred to a thousand head, on two thousand acres of your own land, with an additional thirty thousand leased for summer grazing."

"Very impressive. As George is sicker than a dog this morning, this is your big chance to come with me to a livestock auction."

"George is sick?"

"Stomach flu. So, will you come with me?"

"I can't," she said. "First, there's Mrs. Murphy—"

"I'd rather go with you."

"No, I mean is she up to another day with both children? She looked exhausted yesterday. And how about the responses to your babysitting ad?"

"How about the answering machine?"

She bit her lip as she frowned into her mug. He girded himself. When she looked back at him, the playfulness had fled from her gaze. She finally said, "I'm here to help you find a babysitter, remember? And to help Mrs. Murphy with the kids during the break until we hire someone else. For that I am getting free room and board. I'm not here to date the boss."

"Can't you think of it as a perk?" he said lightly. When she scowled at him, he added, "Mrs. Murphy is taking the kids to see their paternal grandparents today, and then she's getting a perm. I take it that is an all-day affair. Paul Avery has orders to stick to the kids like glue." He met her gaze. "I think it's obvious we're learning how to mix business with pleasure."

She smiled at last. "Yeah, I guess that is kind of obvious."

He kissed the curve of her neck. "How soon can you be ready?"

"It depends," she said softly, and as she twisted to set aside the mug, the sheet slid down to her waist.

He caught her bare shoulders and lowered his head to run his tongue around each perfect nipple. A minute later he was undressed and sliding between the sheets beside her.

HE DECIDED TO TAKE George's old truck, the one with the canopy on the back, as he intended to stop by the feed store after the auction. He threw a tarp in the back in case the canopy leaked, all the while listening to the Avery brothers telling him what to look for at the auction. The predicted snow had not yet arrived, just icy rain the wind drove through every crevice.

They stopped at the diner for a quick breakfast. Trip hadn't really expected to find Marnie waiting tables, but her absence seemed to cast a pall over the place. The waitress who showed up at their table knew Trip and lowered her voice as she took their orders.

"It's so weird in here. The cops have been questioning everyone. Marnie got into an argument with a customer over his bill day before yesterday. He thought she'd cheated him, and you know Marnie, she doesn't suffer creeps quietly." Her eyes clouded over. "Now I hear they had him down at the station half the night. Is that true?"

"I don't know," Trip admitted. He'd purposefully not called the sheriff's office because this wasn't his case, and it was hard enough keeping his nose out of it as it was. He sure as hell wasn't going to get involved with Police Chief Novak. Nevertheless, he heard himself say, "Who are they questioning?"

"A guy named Peter Saks. Do you know him?"

Trip caught Faith's small gasp of recognition. He said, "I've met him," and recalled Torrence saying Saks had been throwing his weight around the diner a couple of days ago.

"There's a rumor his girlfriend is missing, too.

My husband is taking me to work and picking me up. He doesn't want me wandering around alone." She looked toward the kitchen and added, "I'd better take your order. What'll you have?"

They both ordered. The food arrived hot and fresh, but their appetites had vanished. Back in the truck they drove to the auction yard in near silence until Faith said, "If Peter Saks is running around hurting people, then it doesn't seem very likely we have to worry about Neil Roberts and Gene Edwards, does it?"

"No," Trip said. He'd been thinking this, too. After all, there was nothing that pointed to them actually coming after Trip. Perhaps this all had been one coincidence after another and the fugitives were either out of the country by now or dug down deep somewhere waiting out the FBI.

They'd have a long wait.

"The FBI has expanded the search," he added. "No leads on the Idaho agent's murder. I can't imagine why either one of them would bother Marnie Pincer."

From the corner of his eye, he watched as Faith wrapped her arms around herself as if to ward off a sudden chill. "Remember how you told me I'm pretending to be a rancher?" he mused.

"Yes," she said, smiling uneasily. "I'm sorry about that."

"No, you were right on the money. I think ranching is in your blood or it isn't. Face it, it's not in mine. But for today and as many days as I need to, I can act the part and do what needs to be done. Let's concentrate on that for now, okay?"

"Fine with me," she said.

The auction yard itself was crowded with hopeful buyers. Trip had been there before, with his father, but never alone and never to bid on live-stock. He parked at the edge of the crowded lot and the two of them walked to the auction barn. He had an hour in which to inspect the bull.

The animal came with a veterinarian health cer-tificate and a breeding pedigree. There were a couple of other ranchers looking the bull over, one Trip recognized as an old friend of his father's. Trip tried to read the older man's reaction and decided he would bid only if his dad's crony bid, because despite the crash course, the truth was he wasn't ex-perienced enough to judge an animal by himself.

After finding out when his bull was on the docket, he and Faith found a place in the crowded bleachers, and for the next two hours listened as the rain pelted the metal roof high overhead. They cuddled together against the chill wind that blew through the cracks, sipping coffee and hot choco-late bought at the refreshment stand, doing their best to stay warm. It felt like a vacation to Trip, a time away from worry. He'd received a cell phone call from Paul Avery, so he knew Mrs. Murphy and the children were safe, the ranch house was guarded better than most prison yards and Faith was right beside him.

The auctioneer's robotic chants, the murmurs of the mostly male crowd and the sounds of the animals as they paraded in and out of the central ring just added to the oasis of privacy he felt with Faith. He tried to let go of other concerns that weren't really his, and concentrate on her. She'd yielded to him, true; she was a wonderful lover and a great companion, but she'd made it clear in a dozen small ways that she was determined to stand alone.

"I noticed you flinched that day at the school when I asked you if you had children," he said at one point. "Back the first time we met."

She stared into her almost empty mug and whispered, "I may not be able to have a baby."

"Because of your injuries."

"Yes. It's just a possibility, you know. Nothing definite."

"But it hurts."

"Of course it does. I love kids."

"I have two," he said, smiling.

She stared at him a second, shook her head and leaned her shoulder into his, smiling.

His bull was finally announced and they moved closer to the ring in order to bid. His dad's old friend was there, too, but in the end, Trip prevailed and he got a respectful nod from the old friend.

A half hour later he'd arranged payment as well as transport. "Now the feed store," he said, as they walked back to the truck. The rain had turned to snow that didn't stick, and Faith's face acquired a lovely pink sheen from the cold. He kissed her nose before helping her climb into the truck.

"I don't know," she said, as she turned up the heater, "but maybe ranching could be fun."

"Maybe," he said, though he knew it would never satisfy him the way police work did.

"Did you ever like it?"

"You mean when I was a kid?"

"You were born on the ranch, weren't you?"

"Well, in a hospital, but if you mean is the ranch where I grew up, yes, you're right. My little sister was the one who lived and breathed horses and wide-open skies and could never imagine another life."

"But you could."

"Absolutely. Much to my father's chagrin. At first I wanted to be a lawyer, but after graduation I gravitated to law enforcement. It about killed poor old dad. The only thing that saved him was that by then Susan had met Sam Matthews, and Dad loved

Sam." A shadow crossed his face. "Right after they got married, Dad was in a car accident and he died a few weeks later. Sam and Susan helped my mother with the ranch, and when she became ill, took over the place."

"Your mother died this summer?" she asked, holding her hands up to the heater. The escaping air blew her hair in a very beguiling way.

He nodded. "Yeah. She was in a nursing home, kind of holding her own—and then she just died. Everyone was kind of surprised. Luckily, I'd been to see her just a few days before, so I got to say goodbye."

"That was the trip where you got involved with the bus accident."

"Yes. And then a month or so after that, when I was back in Miami and getting ready for an undercover assignment, I got news Susan and Sam were burned to death in a barn fire. Things changed overnight."

"I guess I don't understand who started rebuilding the barn."

"George Plum. He had authorization to continue ranch chores. As soon as the barn was cleared by the fire marshall, George bulldozed the charred remains, determined to make things the way they were. When I got here and saw what he was doing I put the brakes on. I don't want the kids to grow up with a new barn over the spot their folks died. I'm going to make it into an orchard or a garden or something life-affirming."

"I think that sounds lovely," she said, looking at him with a warm glow in her eyes. Had a woman ever regarded him that way before?

"My father would think it was a waste of good land and overly sentimental," he said.

"So? You're not your father's son, I guess."

"I guess not."

They were almost to the edge of town. Trip saw flashing red and blue lights ahead and slowed down as he recognized the police car pulled off the road on the other side of the highway, right behind a familiar old white Mercury. A passing truck and trailer blocked his view until he was past. He glanced into the side-view mirror. A deputy and David Lee stood on the verge.

"Did you see that?" he asked Faith as she seemed to be craning to look in her side mirror as well.

"Was that David Lee?"

"Yeah. I wonder if they finally pinned something on him."

"Wouldn't that be nice," Faith said flippantly, but as he glanced at her, she raised her hand to her face and continued the journey to smooth her hair. It was the first time he'd seen her make that gesture in days.

A few minutes later, he pulled up to the loading

gate of the feed store and went inside to place the ranch order for dietary supplements and supplies to be delivered on Monday. Though it didn't take long, he was so curious about what was going on with David Lee he could barely concentrate. He picked up a bag of rolled oats for Buttercup and left the store as soon as he could.

Faith got out of the truck when she apparently saw him coming with the grain bag slung over one shoulder. She darted around to the back, opened the gate and threw up the canopy door.

"Shall I push this tarp aside?" she called.

"No, spread it out in case the truck bed is wet."

"What about what's inside it?"

"There's nothing inside it," he told her as he strode past the driver's door.

She peeked her head around the left side and said, "Yes there is. Something is rolled up in the green one. Here, I'll just pull it free."

She ducked back around as he breasted the rear of the vehicle and looked inside, confused about the tarp because it should have been blue and folded, not green and rolled. It didn't make sense.

In the next instant, Faith managed to push and shove a corner of green canvas away revealing a hank of long red hair wrapped around a woman's head. The faint odor of decay wafted past his face as Faith screamed.

He dropped the grain sack and caught Faith as she stumbled backward toward the loading dock, workers from inside spilling out as the hair slipped away from the dead woman's face.

Gina was no longer missing.

Chapter Twelve

Faith sat in the feed store, wrapped in a heavy blanket the owner had found somewhere. It smelled strongly of moldy hay, but she didn't care.

If she strained her neck and twisted her head, she could look out the window and see Trip standing with his back to her. Surrounded by lawmen, he was the only one not in a uniform, and yet commanded attention just by the way he stood, the quiet way he listened, his focus.

It was much easier to think about Trip than that poor woman in the back of the truck. Faith covered her mouth as bile pushed up her throat. She'd never forget Gina's waxy white skin or the filmy gaze of her eyes.

At least now they knew what had happened to the babysitter. But who had killed her and how had her body wound up in Trip's truck?

"Can I get you something, miss?" the owner asked. He was a short man with a double chin and a receding hairline. He couldn't quite hide his excitement at all the commotion happening around him.

She stood up and shook off the blanket, folded it and handed it back to him. She'd answered questions for the sheriff, the first to show up, and then from the chief of police. She was tired, and the beginnings of a headache throbbed in her temples. But she was tired of not knowing what was happening, and steeled herself to go back outside.

"I'm fine," she told the owner, "thanks for everything." The wind caught the door when she opened it and she pulled her hood up around her face. Snowflakes were beginning to stick to the pavement. As she walked across the slushy parking lot, an ambulance siren split the afternoon air, and a second later the vehicle itself pulled into the parking lot. The police waved it over to Trip's truck.

Trip turned to watch the ambulance's approach and saw Faith. He immediately started out to meet her, catching her shoulders when he was close enough. "Faith—" he began but she cut him off.

"Don't try to protect me, Trip. I have to know what's going on. Do they know how she died?"

"It's unclear. There's a cut-off rope around her neck and ligature marks around her throat and the one wrist the coroner could see. They won't unwrap her from the tarp until they get her to the morgue."

"Then she was tied up?"

"It looks like it."

"How did she get free and how did she wind up in George's truck? She wasn't alive when she was put in there, was she?" The image of a sick or drugged woman suffocating while they drove around was too dreadful to live with.

"No, she's been dead for a while. Not four days, so the question is where was she kept and why."

They both fell silent as EMTs moved the body bag from the back of Trip's truck onto a gurney and into the back of the ambulance. Snowflakes glittered against the black plastic.

"I called Paul to come get you," Trip said. "The police are going to impound this truck."

"What about you?"

"I'll stick around and catch a ride with the sheriff." He pulled his Stetson even lower on his brow and shoved his bare hands into his pockets. "I don't understand why the killer chose this truck to dump her body."

"Did George know her? Was this aimed at him?"

"I don't know. He tends to drive this truck, but it has a Triple T logo on the door, and any number of people use it."

"So, who knew you were going to the auction instead of George?"

"Everyone on the ranch and everyone related to everyone on the ranch. It wasn't a secret."

"But you just found out this morning."

"No, I knew last night. I just didn't mention it to you. Frankly, I got a little distracted."

He smiled and she remembered the lovemaking that had been the distraction. "I told Mrs. Murphy about our plans and she told Colin and Noelle's grandparents," Trip added. "Who knows who they told."

"Remember when Peter Saks said Gina had a crush on you? If he hurt her, might he stick her body in your truck to either implicate you or shove his power over her in your face?"

"It's possible," he said. "This was risky. I mean, think about it. Gina's body wasn't in the back of the truck this morning at the ranch, and you would have felt someone put her in there if it was done here at the feed store because you were sitting in the cab. That means she was dumped while we were at the restaurant or at the auction yard. Either place had lots of traffic and it had to take a few minutes to do the transfer."

"Then maybe someone saw something. Maybe a security camera picked something up. Wait, didn't the waitress this morning say Peter Saks was in custody?"

"No, she said he'd been questioned. Chief Novak had nothing to hold him on. If there are security tapes, we'll find them. I mean, the police will find them."

"Yes," she said, once again aware of how big a part crime played in Luke Tripper's life.

"This is a rural town," he added, "full of wide-open and desolate places where a body could be stashed with little risk. But instead the killer went to all the trouble to put her where someone from the Triple T, probably me, would find her."

A chill ran down Faith's spine. In the end, she'd been the one to find the poor woman. She met Trip's gaze.

"I won't let anything happen to you," he said and she could see he believed it. But things happened and murderers didn't play by the rules. She instantly chastised herself. Who knew these facts better than Trip?

"There's one man who wants to get back at you," Faith said softly. "Neil Roberts. What if he's here somewhere?"

"I don't think a stranger could hide in a town this small for this long," Trip said. "Plus this isn't Roberts's signature."

"What do you mean? I thought at least one of the women disappeared from her car."

"That's his M.O. His method of operation. That can change as circumstances and experience change. But his reason to kill and what he needs to take from the kill psychologically, that stays constant." He continued bluntly. "Roberts likes to sodomize and then he likes to stage. Gina wasn't presented the way Roberts presents a corpse. Trust me on this. This doesn't feel like his work."

Faith looked down at her feet. She wasn't used to having this kind of conversation, and the semi-detached tone of Trip's voice alarmed her. Every broken bone she'd suffered, every internal organ that had been smashed and repaired, even the scars on her face and body throbbed with reawakened memories of their own.

"Chief Novak said his deputy stopped David Lee today for speeding," Trip said. "He's got an outstanding warrant so they took him to jail."

Too many scary men, too many unknown motives, too many threats. One dead woman, one missing. Faith needed to get away. When the ambulance pulled out of the parking lot it seemed to signal a change. Everyone grew restless; a tow rig backed up to Trip's truck.

As another vehicle bearing the Triple T logo rumbled into the lot, Trip moved closer and lowered his voice. Snow had gathered on the brim of his hat, on the wide breadth of his shoulders. "The kids' grandparents offered to keep them tonight. Mrs. Murphy is going to go stay with her aunt. Let me get you a hotel room."

"No."

"But—"

"No, please, I'll be fine. The ranch is a fortress, just let me go home with Paul Avery. I'll lock myself in my cabin. My head is throbbing—I just want to be alone for a while."

He studied her. "Faith, I wish you'd let me—"

Sheriff Torrence turned from the other men and said, "Trip, can I get you to come back over here and give us your opinion on something?"

Novak glared at Trip. "We don't need—"

"Yes, Chief, we do," Torrence interrupted.

"You go ahead," Faith said.

"Faith, listen to reason."

She put a hand on his cheek for the briefest of moments, aware the combined law enforcement of Boyton County was watching. "I need to get away from all this, Trip, and I can't accept more charity."

The door of the Triple T truck opened. Faith didn't look back as she crossed the lot and climbed into the cab.

THE RATTLE OVER THE cattle guard was beginning to signal home for Faith, and this time, when that thought crossed her mind, she didn't fight it. Home was where you hung your hat, and for now this was it. Paul dropped her off at the cabin and she watched his taillights disappear toward one of the outbuildings.

The ranch house looked kind of forlorn, with no lights glowing from within, no sounds of children or Mrs. Murphy. An armed guard strolled past and murmured a greeting. It was snowing harder on the ranch than it had been in town, due, no doubt, to the higher elevation. Several inches had gathered atop fence posts and porch railings.

Faith let herself into the cabin and locked the door. The view of the construction outside the window reminded her there were more dangers to be reckoned with than an intruder. A well-placed match and the cabin would go up like kindling.

There was no point dwelling on such morbid thoughts, and she closed the drapes against the twilight. A blinking red light on the phone signaled messages and, with a pang, she recalled she was supposed to be hiring a babysitter.

First things first. The cabin did not have a bathtub, but it did have a shower. She stripped off her clothes and stood under the hot water until she was as pink as a tourist on her first day in the tropics. She dressed in warm sweats and dried her hair, letting it fall forward on her face to add additional warmth. Even with the thermostat turned way up, she couldn't seem to get warm.

The first call was from her brother, Zac. Faith listened to both what he said and what he didn't say. On the surface he was telling her he and Olivia and all four babies would leave the next day to fly to Hawaii for the wedding.

Underneath, she could hear Zac's concern and guilt. Guilt his life was working so well and hers wasn't; concern that she was okay. The background sounds of fussing babies and Olivia's voice calling Zac to lunch just made Faith all the more homesick.

She called him back, keeping her voice light and the conversation general. He was excited about the coming trip and she once again assured him she was too busy to get away. She couldn't tell if he knew she was hiding something—she hoped not—and they stopped talking after a few minutes.

The next five messages were hopeful babysitter applicants, and she sat at the counter making notes of their telephone numbers. Once the news of Gina's death hit the morning paper, would any of these women show up for an appointment?

The last call had been placed while Faith was in the shower and it was a familiar voice.

"This is your lucky day," Ruby Lee said around the clatter of ice cubes in a glass. "It's a hell of a lot more than you deserve, that's for sure. I got me a new renter lined up, but he wants the place first thing tomorrow. Get your stuff out of here by ten o'clock tonight and I'll give you a refund." The click of the phone served as a punctuation mark.

A refund meant money and money meant independence. She did some quick calculations in her head and felt one of the bands of worry loosen a little. She hated being almost broke and without options. The refund wasn't a fortune, but it would help.

It was dark, though. She only had two or three hours to make this happen. David was in jail. Faith knew she could be in and out of there in less than an hour if she got Ruby to help her get the one heavy chest into the back of a truck.

She grabbed her coat, gloves and a knit hat. Using the key Trip had given her, she entered the ranch house and went to the laundry area where the well-marked keys to the various ranch vehicles were stored in a cabinet. She chose those to Trip's truck because it was parked right out front and had big old tires with studs in them. She wrote him a note in case he got home before she did.

For a second she paused by the phone. The prudent thing to do would be to call him and ask him to meet her there. Barring that, she could wander around outside until she ran into one of the ranch hands and get them to come with her. The memory of the uncomfortably silent trip back with Paul Avery stopped her. Or maybe it was the last shattered vestige of pride that reminded her she wanted so much to stand alone.

It was a truckload of furniture, for heaven's sake. She made up her mind as she locked the door behind her. Once inside the truck, she popped in one of the CDs she found in a case, expecting country and western music to go with the cows and the ranches she drove past, getting instead Tchaikovsky. Listening to the stirring orchestration was oddly soothing, like listening to a raging storm while tucked safely into a warm bed.

It was also haunting music. She thought of Trip listening to it as he drove to and from the ranch, a fish out of water, drawn back to a life he'd purposely left behind. She thought of him trying so hard to do what was right despite his inclinations and his heart. Tears burned her eyes. Tears for lost dreams, but also tears of respect for the courage it took to play the cards life dealt.

The tears blurred oncoming traffic and she pulled the truck into the diner parking lot. Images of Trip bombarded her. Little vignettes. The first time she'd seen him, standing in the classroom, holding Colin. Reading to Noelle. Stroking Butter-cup. The way he looked and talked, the way he made love and held her. His humor, his wit, his steady gaze…

A smile tugged on her lips and she peered across the dark cab, almost expecting to find him staring back. The day had started out so perfectly, the time in his arms breathtaking and exciting. The auction had actually been fun. Learning about his family had revealed more of his past. Everything had been going along so well until poor Gina.

But sympathies for Gina and ugly images aside, there was no denying one basic truth: she cared for him deeply.

She reached for her shoulder bag and dug in the depths until her hand closed over her cell phone. She didn't use it very often and tended to forget to charge it, so she was relieved to find it had battery power. Still, she hesitated making that call.

What, exactly, did being independent mean, and why was she having such a hard time defining it? She'd borrowed Trip's truck, so why was it difficult to admit she wanted to borrow his time? Why did it seem weak and selfish?

It was dark outside. It was cold and she was on edge. Was it wrong to crave his presence, given the day they'd shared?

She placed the call and settled back in the seat.

His message machine clicked on without delivering a single ring. Suddenly shy, she told him where she was headed and that she would see him later at the ranch. And she knew when she did see him it would be different. Not for him—things hadn't changed for him—but they had for her.

A few minutes later she drove past Ruby Lee's house. The lights were on. She drove slowly, scanning the driveway and street parking for a sign of David's old car, relieved when she didn't see it. She circled the block and at the last minute decided not to alert her landlady she'd come to collect her things. Instead, she'd load up and present the move as a fait accompli. She all but coasted down the steep drive, the truck handling what little snow had accumulated with no problem.

The apartment was as she'd left it—dank and depressing. She could barely wait to get out of there. She turned on every light in the place, banishing shadows.

There were a half-dozen pieces of furniture: a rocking chair, two small tables, a bookcase, a lightweight pine desk and the last piece, a chest of drawers. Making several trips, she loaded everything but the chest into the truck. After a few test lifts, she decided she could manage the chest by herself if she took the drawers out first.

Pushing and shoving the main part of the chest,

she slid it across the linoleum floor. The threshold at the front door took some maneuvering, but once outside it was a short trip to the open gate of the truck.

The thing weighed a ton. What she needed was a rope, and she'd seen one in the tool closet. She went back inside the apartment and through the rooms, checking to see if she'd forgotten anything.

The closet was in the back bedroom, which she'd used for storing boxes and furniture. Now that she knew what to look for, she easily found the door leading to the inside staircase, hidden behind a false panel just as Trip described. She left the panel open to expose the door. She wanted Ruby and David to know she knew about it.

The rope appeared long enough to do the trick, so she grabbed the coil off the hook. As she turned back into the room, the lights went out. Not just in the bedroom, but all through the apartment, plunging it into darkness. Adjoining houses, glimpsed through windows, appeared unaffected.

"A fuse," she mumbled. The fuse box was literally right behind her in the tool closet. She grappled around for a few minutes, but it was so dark she couldn't see anything and was afraid to start pushing random switches.

She'd seen a flashlight in the truck glove compartment. She was trying hard to stay calm, but the sudden darkness and silence had her spooked, and she gripped the rope between both hands as she cautiously made her way toward the bedroom door.

Two steps later, she collided with the precariously stacked drawers and stubbed a toe. "Damn!" she said, her voice sounding unnaturally loud in the all-but-empty room. Limping now and irritated as well as spooked, she felt her way into the hall.

A noise up ahead froze her at midstep. The sound of cloth brushing against cloth. The sound of an exhaled breath. She looked toward the ambient light coming through the large window in the main living area. The outside porch light was off, too. "Ruby?" she said.

No response.

"Ruby? Is that you?"

Nothing.

Maybe it was her imagination. Maybe it wasn't.

She took another step, straining to hear. Still detecting nothing, she picked up her pace. The outside door was just a few steps away. She could get the flashlight. Hell, she could lock herself in the truck and sit there all night if she had to. Her purse and phone were out there…the keys. Her heart hammered so loudly she could barely hear herself think. She was moving on instinct, all senses alert.

Thank goodness David was in jail.

He was, wasn't he?

The door wasn't far ahead now, a shining gray rectangle, the truck a big, hulking shape beyond. A few more steps to safety.

And then she heard it again, this time from behind, as though whoever it was had stood silently as she passed.

Before she could turn, a rock hard arm caught her around the neck, a cloth covered her face. She screamed, but there was no sound. She struggled but felt herself sagging. What was wrong with her, why wasn't her body responding? She was falling.

She hit the floor without feeling a thing.

Chapter Thirteen

"I told you I would never hurt Gina, I loved her," Peter Saks said. He sat at a table in the small, windowless nook that passed as the Shay police department interrogation room. Chief Novak was conducting the proceedings but Sheriff Torrence was there, too, and he'd insisted Trip be allowed entry.

Saks held his head in his hands, his previous bravado absent. Trip did his best to disappear into the wall and leave things to the two official lawmen. He watched Saks with a critical eye, trying to detect how good an actor he was.

"I loved her," Saks repeated, looking up at Novak. His gaze slid to Trip. "Her body was in *his* truck. Ask him how she got there."

"Mr. Tripper was never alone long enough to have the opportunity to put Gina Cooke's body anywhere, even in his own truck," Torrence informed him.

Trip found himself very grateful that two or three of the guys had glanced in the truck that morning and could attest it had been empty when it left the ranch. Otherwise he might be trying to come up with an alibi.

Novak circled the table then leaned in close to Saks. "Where's Marnie Pincer?" he asked.

"Marnie Pincer?"

"The waitress at Shay's Diner."

"I know who she is, but I don't know where she is."

"Funny how she disappeared right after you and her got into it at Shay's."

"Now wait a second," Peter Saks said, his body growing rigid. "I never—"

"Did you know her car was unlocked? It looks like someone grabbed her when she went to leave for work. Just like someone grabbed Gina when she stopped for coffee."

"I don't know nothing about Marnie Pincer."

"I tell you what I think," Novak said. "I think when Gina refused to go off with you, you got mad. I think you threw her in your car and took off and then you killed her." His voice turned to steel. "I think you kind of enjoyed killing Gina, so you nabbed Marnie Pincer for a repeat performance. Where is she? Is she still alive?"

"You've got this all wrong. Sure, I waited for

Marnie but that's just because I wanted to apologize for maybe getting her in trouble with her boss. I didn't hurt her. I even saw her drive away from the restaurant."

Saks had waived his Miranda right to keep silent. When would it would occur to him to stop talking and demand legal representation?

"I never hurt Marnie and I sure as hell didn't lay a hand on Gina."

"My guess is you brought Gina's body back here so you could try to blame everything on Luke Tripper. Am I right?"

"I'm not saying anything else," Saks said, closing his mouth with a visible snap.

"You don't have to," Novak sneered. "I got me a warrant. We're going to tear your place apart. We'll trace the tarp, we'll find your DNA on Gina, maybe we'll even find Ms. Pincer out at your place. God help you if we do."

Peter Saks was as good as his word—he refused to open his mouth. Novak called in his deputy. Lenny took the handcuffed Saks out of the room and, as Torrence and Novak exchanged a few words, Trip followed Lenny, thinking he'd check in on Duke.

But Duke was no longer in a cell; he must have made bail or transferred out. The more alarming fact was David Lee wasn't there, either. Once he and Lenny had left the cell block, Trip said, "I thought you guys arrested David Lee."

"We did, but his mom got him out. He left two hours ago."

"How many times are you going to let him go?"

"The Chief says Lee is just a troublemaker, nothing to worry about, not when we got us a real murderer."

At that moment Torrence appeared. "Trip, you want a ride out to your ranch?"

"Yeah," Trip said. A restless, uneasy feeling was growing in his chest. It wasn't an entirely new sensation. He'd felt it before—when he was undercover, when he was pretty sure someone was on to him. But that wasn't the case now. He didn't know what to attribute this feeling to, except that Gina was dead and Faith didn't answer her phone.

Nate Pincer was striding across the parking lot as Trip and Torrence exited the station. The snow that had started earlier was sticking now, and it was still coming down. The wind had picked up, too.

Pincer rushed toward Torrence with single-minded passion. Grabbing the sheriff's sleeve, he demanded to know what was being done to find his wife.

In his anxiety, Pincer knocked Torrence's hat from his bald head. The sheriff retrieved it and pulled it back on as he said, "Mr. Pincer, calm down, sir."

"I don't trust Novak," Pincer said.

"He has a suspect," Torrence replied.

Trip had seen his share of frightened relatives of victims. Nate Pincer looked the part. Unshaven, wrinkled, almost dusty despite the weather, he seemed to be shrinking in front of them. Trembling, he said, "Our son is on his way home from college…you've got to do something."

"By this time tomorrow, sir, the place will be crawling with law enforcement. Go home. Let us work on this. Get some sleep."

"I heard about the Cooke girl," Pincer said. "What if there's a serial killer in town? What if he grabbed my Marnie?" He moved off without an answer, flinging open the station door so hard it crashed against the wall.

"He's got a point," Torrence said as he unlocked the squad car and got behind the wheel. "Trouble is, I happen to know he and Marnie got into a fight before he left on his last trip."

"He claimed they hadn't," Trip said, but now he recalled Nate's pause.

"Told me he was embarrassed to admit it. Said it was no big deal."

Trip was scanning the calls he'd missed while inside with the others. Novak had insisted on no cell phones interrupting his interrogation.

"Dumb obstinacy is not good in a lawman,"

Torrence said, as he started the car and pulled away from the curb. "Novak has settled on Peter Saks."

"He settled on Saks days ago."

"Exactly."

"I tried to talk to him—"

"He resents you. He's never investigated a murder before, and he's not going to listen to me, either. It'll be out of his hands tomorrow, though. All I need to do is keep him from impeding things tonight."

"Better you than me," Trip said.

Trip bypassed a message from Colby to listen to one left by Faith. Something in her voice brought a smile to his lips until the content sank in—she was on her way to the Lee household to pick up her furniture. "Turn around," he said suddenly. "Drive to the Lee house."

"But—"

"Faith thinks Lee is in jail, but he isn't—he's been out for two hours. She's over at his place now." As Trip spoke, Torrence made a U-turn. Trip punched in Faith's number as the car screeched out of the curve and sped back into town. The phone flipped over to messages after two rings. Trip hung up and swore.

"Go faster," he urged. "Hurry."

The feeling in his chest suddenly had a name: Faith.

They arrived at the Lee house within ten minutes but they were a long ten minutes to Trip. There was no sign of Lee's car parked at the curb. Torrence turned in to the driveway, the headlights bouncing as they headed down. While there were lights on in the top part of the house, the basement was dark. Trip's truck was parked outside, the tailgate open, a chest of drawers ready to load, everything sporting a scattering of newly fallen snow.

Trip was out of the car before it stopped. The front door of the basement apartment stood wide open but the light switch didn't work. Torrence's headlights illuminated some of the place, but not enough for a good search. Trip dashed back to the truck and opened the door, which activated the cab lights and set off the key alert chime. Faith's purse and cell phone were on the passenger seat. He reached past the steering wheel, grabbed the keys out of the ignition and retrieved the flashlight.

The main living area was empty. Calling Faith's name, he moved through the small rooms and found nothing out of place except for a stack of drawers in the small room. The door to the closet was open as was the sliding panel. The inside door itself was locked from the other side.

"You find anything?" Torrence asked as he entered the room wielding a flashlight of his own.

"Nothing." On their way out, Torrence flashed

a light into the bathroom, but Trip kept going into the living room. His flashlight had revealed a coil of rope on the floor. He knelt to pick it up.

"That rope mean anything to you?" Torrence said.

"No. Anything in the bathroom?"

"Nope."

"Let's get upstairs and see if the landlady knows what's going on."

They started out the door, Torrence leading the way. It was impossible to see any tracks on the ground, as it was a muddy, snowy mess. Trip held back for a second, trying to figure out where Faith could have gone. The logical assumption was that something had happened to the lights and she'd left the apartment to go ask the landlady for help. Maybe she didn't know about the flashlight in the glove box of the truck.

It didn't feel right.

He started off again, but paused as he detected a noise on the hillside at the back, up toward the row of houses on the other side. He swept the flashlight on the wooded area, but the falling snow precluded seeing much of anything except occasional glimpses of a path. As he stared, something moved on the path.

He immediately took off at a dead run. The noise in the bushes got loud enough to hear over the wind whipping the trees overhead. He reached for his gun and realized he wasn't carrying it, he hadn't put it on that morning when he left the house for a day at the auction.

A day with Faith.

What if he was chasing a bunch of kids out on a winter night escapade, or a homeowner looking for a dog? What if Faith was at her landlady's house?

What if she'd been snatched away like Gina and Marnie?

He ran harder.

The trail was steep and slippery with icy mud, and he was encumbered by a heavy jacket. Pushing branches out of the way, he ran mostly blind.

He finally stopped for a second to get his bearings and listen again. He heard more crashing noises, heavy breathing that wasn't his own. Grabbing at slippery rocks and tree limbs to traverse the rain-gullied path, he climbed steadily until a grunt and an oath were followed by a dark shape hurtling down the bank, headed right for him. He shined the light upward and caught sight of a shining halo of gold.

Faith's hair.

Running fast now, scrambling on all fours when necessary, he tried to reach her before she hit the ground. He wasn't fast enough. Her body crashed up ahead and immediately began rolling, the lifeless, soundless way it moved constricting his heart.

He caught her as she flew off the edge of the path. Her weight threw them both to the ground, but at least this time his body cushioned her fall—if she was alive to feel anything.

Before he could roll her over and get to his feet, more crashing announced another body hurtling down the path, but this one was on its feet. A man wearing a stocking mask jumped over Trip and Faith and continued down the hill.

Trip let him go. He gently rolled Faith onto her back. He was vaguely aware of lights and shouting at the bottom of the hill, but he ignored them, concentrating on Faith.

He shined a light on her muddy, bloodied face, smoothing her hair away from her eyes and mouth. His breath condensed into a cloud of vapor, shrouding her face—or maybe it was the tears in his eyes that blurred her features.

"Hold on," he urged, leaning over and kissing her forehead, putting his freezing fingers against her throat where he found a heartbeat. Her eyelids fluttered and he moved the light so it wouldn't blind her, but her eyes didn't open. She was either drugged or hurt, or maybe both. He dug in his pocket for his cell phone but before he could flip it open, he heard sirens in the distance and Torrence yelling at him.

FAITH AWOKE WITH A monumental headache and a dry mouth. Where was she?

She recognized the smells and sounds, the hushed urgency. A hospital.

For a second, she was in Westerly. She'd been hit by a car; she hurt everywhere. Where was her father? Where were Zac and Olivia? She heard a noise to her left and turned her head too fast. The room spun, her stomach lurched. She closed her eyes and took shallow breaths and within a few seconds the sensations lessened to where she could handle them. She opened her eyes.

A man lay sprawled on a chair. At first she thought he was Zac, and then he opened his eyes. Not blue like Zac, but velvety brown. His nose hadn't been broken, he was heavier, darker.

"Trip?" she whispered.

He was at her side in an instant. "I'm here."

She looked around slowly, trying to remember.

"You're going to be okay," he added. "How are you feeling?"

"Like hell," she murmured.

"Do you remember what happened to you?" His voice was soft and his eyes glowed as though worry burned his brain.

"Faith?"

"I… I don't know for sure," she said, the effort of trying to think almost too much.

"Later—" he began.

"The lights went out," she said. She could recall the terror of the dark rooms. "Someone was there."

"Someone cut the wires to the apartment," Trip said.

"It was dark." Her hands flew to her throat. "He grabbed me."

"Did you see who it was? Could you tell by his voice?"

"He didn't speak," she said. She could feel the beginnings of the shakes way deep inside, and she willed them to stay hidden. "I couldn't see him. He put a cloth over my face."

"He drugged you. Then he picked you up and carried you up the hill. Do you remember any of that?"

She shook her head, which was ill-advised. Again her stomach flip-flopped and her vision blurred.

"Do you know who it was?" she whispered.

"David Lee."

"You're sure?"

"Torrence caught him at the bottom of the hill."

"Where were you?"

"I was with you," he said, a knot forming in his jaw.

"I don't understand."

"He dropped you as he was trying to escape."

"And you didn't go after him?"

"This can all wait," he said. "You need to get some sleep."

"Are the children safe?"

"They're fine—they're still with their grandparents."

"I want to get out of this hospital," she said, her voice only slightly wavery.

"You're scratched and bruised, and you still have whatever he gave you in your system—"

"I want out of this hospital," she repeated, struggling to sit up. The shakes had burst through her weakened defenses and her hands trembled as she peeled blankets away from her legs. "I can't be here. I can't go through this again."

Tears burned her eyes as she struggled against his gentle but firm restraint. She didn't want to cry. She didn't want to be weak and vulnerable and scared....

"I want out of here. Please, Trip, please don't leave me here."

He sat down on the bed and gathered her into his arms. "Who said anything about leaving?" he murmured, holding her like she was a child, his warm hands pressing her cheek against his chest.

She fell asleep in his arms.

Chapter Fourteen

"He said he parked his car on the street on the other side of the gully because he didn't want the police to know he was at his mother's house." Torrence pushed his hat back on his head and sighed.

"How did he explain the fact he had Faith?" Trip asked.

"Listen to this, you'll love it. He said he was coming down the hill when he heard someone crashing through the brush. He stepped off the path just as a man carrying something over his shoulder approached him. He said the other man panicked and it looked to Lee as though he decided to cut his losses by tossing what he was carrying—which we now know to be Miss Bishop—down the hill. David Lee decided to get the hell out of Dodge while the other man rushed past him."

"Wearing a ski mask?"

"Yeah."

Trip glanced into the hospital room. He knew the sheriff and Chief Novak had both already talked to Faith. She looked exhausted as a nurse's aide helped her into a wheelchair for discharge. He pulled Torrence farther away from the opening and said, "Do you believe him?"

"I didn't until he confessed he ran Miss Bishop off the road several days ago. He admitted he threatened her on the sidewalk. But he swears he didn't have anything to do with this."

"What about letting the air out of her tires?"

"He won't confess to that, either, but I think he's embarrassed because it's such a sophomoric trick."

"What did they find at Faith's apartment and out on that hill?"

"Novak has men out there this morning looking for footprints, processing the scene. But there was more snow during the night and the weather is still deteriorating. He should have done more last night."

"How about the cut wires? That takes some familiarity with the place."

"Normally, yes, but in this case it's all on the outside of the place and it's old—it wouldn't take a genius to figure it out."

The aide rolled Faith out into the hall just then. Trip smiled at her. "I'll catch up," he called, as she and the aide headed for the elevator. Looking back at the sheriff, he said, "Quick now, what did they learn from the autopsy on Gina?"

"It's not scheduled until this afternoon, but we do know a few things. Gina Cooke was tied up, one rope around her neck, another around her wrists and ankles. It looks like she managed to get her hands free and saw off the rope fastened around her neck. Her body is scratched and bruised, lividity revealed she'd been lying on her left side for a while after death, but she wasn't dead for four days, so that means someone around here was keeping her alive."

"There goes Novak's claim that Peter Saks killed her days ago."

"Yeah, but it doesn't let Saks off the hook."

"Did Novak search his place for some sign of Marnie Pincer like he said he was going to?"

"Impounded his car and took his house apart. Nothing yet."

Trip watched as the elevator doors closed. "I have to go," he said. "Keep me posted, okay?"

"Wait. Take a second and tell me what your FBI contact said."

"Colby received a report that two men matching the description of Roberts and Edwards were seen buying gas the day before yesterday about fifty miles south of here."

"Two days ago!"

"Yeah, the information got misplaced. Unfortunately, it happens once and awhile. He also said they've found out that Edwards has an estranged uncle living in Howser. They're mounting a search there in approximately—" he glanced at his watch "—an hour. I'll let you know when I hear something."

He delivered the last line of this as he strode to the door leading to the stairs. Taking them two at a time, he met Faith and the aide on the ground floor.

A minute or two later, he'd retrieved his sister's red sedan and helped Faith inside. Snow swirled through the sky, blew against the car.

"What about the children?" she asked again, as they left the parking lot.

"We're going to go get them."

"Wouldn't they be safer where they are?"

"The Matthews are great people, but they're elderly and they've made it clear they can't take care of the kids for more than a few hours at a time. It was stretching it leaving them there last night." He sighed wearily. "There's no way they can handle an additional night. Mrs. Murphy is back at the ranch by now. She can take care of them."

"I'm not worried about caring for them," Faith said, searching his face. "You know I love them."

"I know. Listen, I've made a decision. Your family is in Westerly, right?"

"No, they left early this morning for Hawaii."

"All of them?"

"Yes."

He swore. "Okay, then we'll do it this way. We'll go home and pack everyone up, and then I'm seeing that you and the kids get away from here before the weather makes that impossible."

"If we're snowed in, then they'll be snowed out, right?"

"I don't know," he said, and that was the truth. He didn't know where they were, or how many of them there were. Hell, he wasn't even sure they were headed here. He glanced at the dashboard clock. The cops should have raided Edwards's relative's house by now. Why didn't Colby call?

"What about you?" Faith asked.

"I'm staying here. I'm seeing this through."

"But—"

"One woman is dead, one is missing. There will be a half-dozen law agencies in Shay by tomorrow. I'll be in good company."

He turned the windshield wipers on high and was glad he'd had the snow tires put on Susan's sedan. For a second, he flashed on his years in Miami, when the closest he got to "snow" was a drug raid. Ah, the good old days.

An hour later, the children were in the backseat, and they headed home to regroup. Noelle was giving a very loud blow-by-blow account of the visit with her grandparents, struggling to be heard over Colin who was protesting his car seat. Faith, whose beautiful face was scratched and bloodied from the tumble down the hill, looked as white as the snow blanketing the countryside.

And was there snow. The roads weren't plowed, and the snow was collecting, making driving increasingly difficult. Add a temperature drop and a howling wind, and he began to wonder if he'd be able to get Faith and the kids away.

Damn! He should have made sure they were gone days ago, but he'd gotten distracted by his growing feelings for Faith and the mess with Gina, and then Marnie, to say nothing of David Lee and Peter Saks.

And now someone had come close to abducting Faith.

The conclusion Trip would like to believe was that David Lee was behind it. He'd been found on the path, he'd threatened her at least twice, and now he was safely locked away. If Lee had tried to take Faith, and Peter Saks had killed Gina and Marnie Pincer got pissed off at her husband and ran off with some undisclosed friend, then no one was in danger anymore.

But it didn't sit well. Three women, all victims of unrelated violence, all within the last few days, all in or near their vehicles at the time? Unlikely. Gina abducted, then murdered. Marnie abducted, fate unknown. Faith abducted, escaped by pure chance.

Signature or no signature, it sounded like Neil Roberts, and that made Trip's gut clench.

THE SNOW CONTINUED, THE wind picked up and the temperature dropped. Faith carried Colin into the house with his head buried against her neck, his little arms gripping her like she was a lifesaver. Trip carried Noelle.

The ranch house was warm, thanks to a fire in the big kitchen grate that George Plum had started. He explained Mrs. Murphy couldn't get her subcompact out to the ranch until the roads were plowed and that half the ranch hands had some version of the stomach flu. Faith was relieved when Trip convinced George to go back to his quarters, as the last thing they needed on top of everything else was to get sick.

Faith, on the other hand, refused to be coddled. She did not want to fall into the role of cosseted victim, a role she'd given up weeks before and had no intention of revisiting. She was relieved that Trip seemed to understand this, relieved he didn't try to get her to sit down or take it easy or pace herself, or any of the other things her father and brother and Olivia had used to try to help.

She needed and wanted to stay busy.

There were more phone messages from wannabe babysitters and Faith dutifully made notes for call-backs when the weather improved.

Trip started making grilled cheese sandwiches while Faith warmed soup for Colin. Noelle sat at the table, coloring in a new book her grandfather had given her, other toys scattered across the tabletop. Colin was in his high chair, kicking Noelle's toys and banging a plastic spoon against her shoulder.

"Daddy? Make Colin stop," Noelle whined.

The word *Daddy* reverberated through the room. Trip put down the cheese slicer and walked over to Noelle, kneeling by her chair until they were eye to eye.

Faith couldn't see his face, but she could see Noelle's, and the little girl looked nervous. She finally whispered, "Is it okay if I call you that, Uncle Trip?"

"Of course it's okay," Trip said, wrapping her in a hug. When Colin whacked him with the spoon, Trip stood up and moved the high chair farther away. The baby squealed in protest. Trip grabbed a box of dry cereal from the shelf and delivered a handful to Colin's tray.

Peace reigned.

"Nicely done," Faith said as he returned to her side. He leaned down and kissed her forehead, his lips lingering for a moment. She found herself yearning for the night.

"I think I'm beginning to win them over," he said. "How about you?"

"What do you mean?"

"Have I won you over?"

"Pretty damn close." She laughed.

He gestured at the little handmade doll Noelle had propped against the crayon box. "Is that the new toy of the week?"

"Yes, Buster is bedtime comfort and this doll is daytime."

"It looks handmade."

"Eddie Reed's mother sent it over for Noelle. Did you know he lives with his mom?"

"I know he drives to and from work. I don't imagine he'll be coming in today."

Faith glanced out the window at the blowing snow. She was glad they were alone in this little oasis, this little island of domesticity. "He and his mother live on a Christmas tree farm over that direction," she said, trying to point in the general direction Eddie had indicated. When Trip, who she finally noticed was distracted, glanced at his watch for the third time in as many minutes, she added, "Why do you keep checking the time?"

His cell phone rang. "This is why," he said, checking the number and leaving the kitchen.

He doesn't want me or the children to hear what he's saying. As she finished making lunch and feeding Colin his soup, the warm, cozy atmosphere began to fade away. What if David Lee was out of jail again? What if he came looking for her? What about Colin and Noelle?

Trip will protect the kids.

And he would protect her, too. It hadn't been lost on her that he'd stayed on the hillside with her instead of chasing David Lee. That must have strained his instincts, but it said something about how much he cared for her.

Of course he cared for her. He showed it in every glance, in every gesture.

He came back into the room, his expression dispelling any last remnants of tranquility. "That was Colby."

"The FBI guy."

"Yeah." He motioned her over to the stove, where he turned his back to the children and kept his voice low. "They raided a house in Howser this morning. That's three or four hours north. It belonged to an uncle of Gene Edwards. I haven't told you, but Edwards and Roberts were seen south of here a couple of days ago."

Faith swallowed. "Did they find some trace of them?"

"The uncle was shot in the head. Dead at least

a day. His car was stolen, his gun cabinet ransacked. They don't know for sure yet what else is missing. They're processing the scene, looking for fingerprints or some proof they were the ones who murdered the old man."

"Then we're back where we started? We don't know if they're on their way to Canada or here?"

He put his arms around her. "No, it's not the same. I *know* it was them. Before it was all so up in the air, but this isn't a coincidence—they're on their way. We have to get everyone out of here right now." He rested his chin on top of her head. "Pack a few clothes for the kids. I'm going out to the barn to tell whoever I can find to take off, then I'm taking you and the kids to safety, weather be damned."

"And you're coming with us?"

"Yes."

She could hardly believe her ears. She stretched up to kiss him, his mouth the warm haven it always was despite the fear gnawing at her bones. "I'm so glad you changed your mind."

He started to move away and she touched his arm. He turned back to her and she said, "I just want you to know I'm grateful."

"Grateful? For what?"

For you, she wanted to say. She shrugged, "You know, for everything."

He stared right into her eyes. "You must know how I feel about you, Faith. I—"

"Not now, not like this," she interrupted. "Later, when we're all safe."

"If that's how you want it," he said, and leaning down, quickly kissed her cheek again.

As the door closed behind him, Faith deposited Colin in his playpen and set Noelle to work choosing three small toys for each of them to take in the truck. She was upstairs packing their clothes and baby things into a duffle bag when an explosion shook the very foundation of the house.

She flew to the window and looked outside.

It had stopped snowing, but one of the big barns was engulfed in flames and the wind blew the flames toward the house. She saw two men emerge from another barn, hurrying toward the fire. One of them was Trip and he was yelling and gesturing with his arms. As she watched, the man a few feet in back of him fell to his knees, red splatters arcing out behind him, staining the snow.

It was Paul Avery.

Trip turned to look at the fallen man. Faith struggled with the window, but Trip had locked it, and in her panic, she couldn't raise the sash. Did he know that Paul had been shot? A new movement caught her eye and she saw yet another man step out of the horse barn, glance around, then take aim at Trip's back.

She knew that face, those dead eyes. Neil Roberts, here, in Shay, at the ranch. In the next instant, she saw the snow puff a few feet in front of Trip from the impact of a bullet.

Looking around for something with which to break the glass so she could shout a warning, she saw Trip draw a gun from the holster inside his waistband and run for cover in the half-built barn. Other men appeared from other buildings, the snow hampering their progress. One more man went down and they scattered.

The fire, meanwhile, seemed to grow in intensity as the human drama played itself out below. She'd seen enough. She raced down the stairs, cursing her decision not to learn how to handle a gun. If she knew how to use a rifle she could break an upstairs window and pick off the bad guys like a movie heroine.

But even if she could actually hit a moving target, it would draw attention to herself and ultimately the children. Could she take the chance of exposing Noelle and Colin to whoever came through the door?

No.

She ran into the den, broke the glass in the gun case and chose a weapon. If she had to, she could shoot someone point-blank. Faced with figuring out which ammunition went with which gun, however, she abandoned that plan and grabbed the phone to call for help. No dial tone. Snagging her handbag off the hall table, she scooped up Colin and grabbed Noelle's hand, running toward the kitchen.

Maybe they could escape out the back, but what then? She mentally reviewed which buildings they could reach without being seen from the front— there was a garden shack back there, but it offered minimal protection. The thought of getting trapped out in the snow with two kids and a gunman was unthinkable and yet the thought of sitting in the house while it went up in flames was just as terrifying.

Trip's sole goal would be to reach them, to protect them. All she could do was keep them safe until he came.

If he came.

Chapter Fifteen

There wasn't time to curse himself or the gods or the FBI. There wasn't time to do anything but get out of the way of flying bullets and try to put out the fire before it reached the house.

But where had these men come from, how had they approached the ranch unheard and unseen?

There wasn't a doubt in his mind who his adversaries were or what they wanted. He had to outsmart them, outlast them, get around them. Paul Avery was dead; another man, he wasn't sure who, was at best wounded.

He found a ladder in the half-constructed barn and used it to gain access to the beam that ran parallel to the ground, staying low, inching along in hopes of reaching a spot he could use as a vantage point for taking out the sniper.

Almost at once, he saw George Plum erupt from his cabin wearing pajama bottoms, boots and a heavy coat. George's gaze was glued to the raging fire, seemingly oblivious to the danger into which he ran.

"Get down, go back!" Trip yelled, flailing an arm, giving away his position but there was no choice. George looked around as though trying to figure out what was going on. A second later, the sharp pop of gunfire resulted in George grabbing his shoulder and spinning to the ground. Another bullet hit the beam by Trip's hip. He rolled off the beam and hit the ground twelve feet later. The two feet of accumulated snow absorbed some of the shock of the fall and he scrambled to his feet quickly, sure the sniper would be coming after him any second.

No, wait. Two bullets, two angles, two snipers.

Through the half-constructed walls, he saw George making his way back toward the relative safety of his cabin as a man's voice yelled, "Luke Tripper? Give yourself up, we don't want nobody else."

Neil Roberts. Probably Edwards, too. The truth was, Edwards and Roberts would kill everyone on this ranch whether Trip came forward or not. At that moment, the most important thing for Trip to do was find better shelter and come up with a plan to get Faith and the kids out of harm's way.

He took off in the opposite direction, toward the back of Faith's cabin, using anything he could as shelter along the way, giving up speed for stealth. Thank goodness for the continued noise of the fire. He came to a dead halt when he saw his destination already occupied by two of his employees standing with hands held over their heads. A third man with his back to Trip held a gun on them.

Hal Avery met Trip's gaze and then looked quickly away as Trip dodged behind the porch railing. The other man was Eddie Reed, who Trip hadn't realized had even come into work that day.

Trip wasn't sure where Roberts was, only that the man holding the gun ten feet away wasn't him. Too short, too stocky. Gene Edwards, maybe.

Trip took a cautious step in the snow. Eddie Reed watched him carefully, and that apparently registered on Edwards, who spun quickly, firing as he turned. His bullets went wild, but Trip's didn't. Gene Edwards went down like a sack of rocks. More gunfire erupted from in back of Trip. His thigh seemed to explode and he sagged. He was barely aware of Hal Avery taking Edward's gun off his body and returning fire as Eddie hauled Trip to safety.

Trip clutched his leg. Blood seeped through his fingers. He dug in his parka pocket for his phone. It was gone, probably lost in the snow when he fell. "Damn," he muttered.

Hal Avery ducked back around the corner.

Trip heard a frantic whinny and looked toward

the horse barn. The fire had reached the roof. Poor Buttercup. The only building standing in the fire's path before it jumped to the house was this cabin. "Anyone got a phone?" he demanded. "We need reinforcements and the fire department."

Neither man carried a cell phone. "There's a water truck in the machine shop," Trip said. "If someone could reach that, we could use it both as a shield and to protect the house."

"I'll go," Hal Avery said. "Bastards killed my brother."

Eddie kneeled by Trip, offering a grease-smudged rag which Trip pressed against his leg. "I have an idea," he said.

Trip listened carefully as Eddie sputtered out details, his nerves making him talk a mile a minute. The plan was dangerous but it could work, and best of all, if it did, it safeguarded Faith and the kids.

The fact was if there were only two gunmen, one dead now, Faith and the kids were safest right where they were. But how did he know for sure how many gunmen there were? And even if it was just Roberts left, who said he wouldn't use Faith and the kids as hostages?

Trip tried to stand but his leg wouldn't support him. He stared hard at Eddie and said, "There's not much snow, you know, you'd have to be very careful."

"I know."

"Okay, Eddie, you try to get to the back of the house, Hal, you get to the machine shop. I'll provide a diversion." He tied the rag around his leg to stem the blood flow and shifted position again.

Hal took off in one direction, Eddie another, as Trip propped himself against the edge of the building and shouted. "Neil? Let's talk about what you want."

"I want you. Simple."

Trip reloaded his gun. "Let's see if we can come up with a different plan," he yelled.

"No negotiation, FBI man," Roberts said. From the sound of his voice, he was moving when he said it.

Trip lay on his belly, clearing the snow out of his way. Looking under the cabin, he got a pretty good view of the front of the house near the parking area. He yelled, "You know this isn't going to end well, Neil."

He saw a movement over by the horse barn. Roberts was making his way toward Trip's position. Trip would never be able to outrun him. He didn't need to outrun him, he just needed to stop him long enough for Eddie to get Faith and the kids out of harm's way and for Hal to get the water truck.

"Ain't going to end well for which one of us?" Roberts hollered, on the move again, veering toward the parked trucks. Even if Trip could lead him and get a shot off, the most he could hit was a leg. That was better than nothing, but it wouldn't entirely neutralize him.

Wait a second! He was running toward the parked cars. The truck had a full tank of gas.

Trip braced his gun hand on a rock and waited.

ARMED WITH A KITCHEN knife, Faith pulled the kids down on the floor under the table where flying glass wouldn't be as likely to hit them.

She dug her cell phone out of her purse. Powered up, it beeped twice, flashed a low-battery message and turned itself off. In frustration, she threw it across the kitchen.

Noelle sobbed softly against her new doll and Faith pulled her closer. She kissed the top of her head. "It'll be okay, honey, I promise."

"Daddy will come for us?"

"Yes, of course he will."

She heard the fire roaring outside, punctuated by explosions. It was hard not to think about Trip's sister and her husband dying in a fire just a few months before in virtually the same spot.

For what seemed an eternity she sat there holding the children, trying to keep Colin from fussing or crawling away, unsure what the noises she heard meant. She almost jumped out of her skin when she heard the rattle of the back door a few minutes later. It had to be Trip. Handing Colin to Noelle, she crawled across the floor, knife in hand, then inched up the wall next to the door. There was a window set into the door and a curtain covering the window.

Good heavens, if it was a madman with a gun, he'd break the window—he wouldn't knock!

She slid the curtain back. Eddie Reed. Taking a deep breath, she held the knife by her leg and opened the door.

Eddie came inside quickly, along with smoke-tinged air.

"You and the kids are supposed to come with me," he said, his gaze darting around the kitchen. Noelle struggled to her feet with Colin dangling in her arms and Faith set the knife down to help her.

"What about Trip and the others?"

Eddie studied Faith's face. Her fingers went to touch her scars and then she remembered all the new scrapes and bruises. No wonder he stared at her. "Mr. Tripper took a bullet," he said. "But he's real worried about you, Miss Bishop."

The air seemed to be sucked out Faith's lungs as she whispered, "Is he hurt badly? I have to go—"

He caught her arm. "I don't know for sure how bad he's hurt. Mr. Plum is down, too. Mr.

Tripper told me to get you and the kids out the back way before it's too late. He's afraid your cabin is going to go up next, and after that, it'll be the house."

As if to punctuate the urgency, Faith heard bullets or explosions or both coming from the front yard. "Miss Bishop?" Eddie said, helping Noelle zip her fluffy coat and boots. "The boss made it pretty clear I'm supposed to get you guys out the back while he keeps the gunmen busy in the front."

Noelle, hooded now, pulled on her mittens. Faith zipped Colin into the snowsuit she'd brought downstairs for him and threw on her own jacket and hat. She grabbed the duffle bag and followed Eddie outside.

"What now?"

"This way. Keep the baby quiet," Eddie said as he picked up Noelle.

Faith held Colin's head against her shoulder as she followed Eddie across the snowy field toward the garden shack. Eddie opened the doors and they all rushed inside. He put Noelle down at once and focused on a snowmobile that took up almost all available floor space, pushing old bags of potting soil and garden tools aside.

"That?" she said. "We're leaving on that?"

"Yeah. I found it my first day here when I looked in all the buildings. I don't think Mr.

Tripper even knew it was here. Oh, and look, it's got a full tank of gas. It's our lucky day, huh?"

"Sure, real lucky. But it's dangerous for children—"

"More dangerous than bullets and fire? Don't worry, it won't be a long ride," he said as he flung the shack door open wide for a getaway.

He'd made his point. Eddie put Noelle behind him, then Faith climbed on behind Noelle, holding a very distraught Colin sandwiched between them. The duffle bag hung from her arm. They took off in a spray of snow, veering away from the house. Faith tried to look back but all she could see was black smoke flicked with flames.

The machine was incredibly loud, the ride bumpy and frightening, mainly because of her overriding fear for the kids and the terrible uneasiness in the wake of abandoning Trip. The snow was still in abeyance, but the wind combined with the speed of the snowmobile sent icy fingers through every gap in her clothing. Conversation of any kind was impossible.

Eventually, the land began to slope upward and the snow got deeper, the wind more harsh. Faith bowed her head to keep the stinging cold from biting the new abrasions on her face and tried not to think about Trip.

But that was impossible. Eddie said he'd taken

a bullet. At least he was conscious and still making decisions, but the thought he could also be bleeding to death tortured her.

She should have told him she loved him. Before he went outside and all hell broke loose, she should have told him what he meant to her and let him tell her whatever it was he wanted to say. If she never got the chance to tell him or hear those words from his lips, she'd regret it forever.

And what would happen to the children if something happened to Trip? She tucked her head against Noelle's and tried to imagine a world without Trip and these two kids, and she just could not.

He circled the hillside which grew increasingly more forested. The ride got choppier, staying aboard trickier, straining her muscles to the breaking point. After an interminable amount of time, they left the forest and crossed a field, then entered an area heavily planted with evergreen trees. All the trees were about the same size and close together, the lower branches shielding much of the ground. There was a uniform and yet ragged appearance to them, like an overgrown crop.

Or an overgrown Christmas tree farm.

The way became easier now, as Eddie guided the snowmobile along a road running alongside the trees, dodging fallen limbs and debris as the wind continued to whip things around. He stopped at long last under a sloping roof attached to a barn opposite a very old, white two-story house. The house was set amid the usual scattering of outbuildings.

The sudden quiet when he turned off the engine was almost deafening. Faith immediately climbed off, stumbling for a moment as her knees wobbled, clutching Colin to her with the fierceness of a mother bear. She was so cold she was numb. Steadying herself, she helped Noelle to her feet.

"You all right, honey?" she asked.

"I'm freezing," the little girl said around chattering teeth.

"I got to thinking the best thing would be to bring you to my house," Eddie said, taking off his gloves. He'd worn the one helmet that had been looped over the handlebars, and that came off next. His expression was as uncomplicated as ever. "Come on inside and I'll make the kids something warm to drink. We can call the cops."

"Okay," Faith said. The truth? She was a little annoyed they'd come so far to get to a phone, when Trip had a closer neighbor by far, but she let it go. What was the point of stewing? They crossed the snowy yard and climbed the porch stairs. As she and Noelle stamped the snow from their shoes, Eddie unlocked the door and gestured them inside.

He closed the door behind them and switched on the lights.

The inside of the house smelled musty and appeared run-down, just like the outside, but it was filled with enough handmade crafts to open a country store. Noelle audibly gasped with wonder as she spied the shelves lined with plush animals, dolls sitting on quilted cushions, their embroidered eyes and lips smiling a welcome. There was a time-out-of-time quality to the room that under ordinary circumstances would have been enchanting.

But while Faith admired the skill and effort necessary to create such a collection, her focus was Trip. "Where's your phone?" she asked as Colin grabbed at her hat. She took the snow-crusted knit hat off and put it atop her coat by the front door.

"In the kitchen," he said. "It's warmer in there, come on."

Faith helped Colin and Noelle out of their icy outerwear before following Eddie through a swinging door. One glance took in a sink full of dirty dishes and cluttered drain boards. Maybe Eddie's mother was so disabled she stayed upstairs, because the kitchen had a definite uncared-for look that was at odds with the parlor.

But it was the phone Faith was desperate to find and she finally spied it on the wall, hanging by the back door. Holding Colin on her hip, she took the phone off the hook. It was an old rotary model she hadn't seen since she was a kid. She dialed 9-1-1 while holding the receiver, turning her body to keep Colin from accidentally disconnecting the call. When she finally got the receiver to her ear, her heart sank.

"The line is dead," she said with a sinking heart.

Eddie was at the stove, heating milk in a saucepan over a gas flame. He looked over his shoulder. "Wind must have knocked a branch down and damaged the line."

Her head roared with white noise. How could she help Trip now? "I need to take your truck into town to get the police."

"Left my truck at the ranch when I brought you and the babies over here," he said. "Let me think a moment."

"How about neighbors?"

"Five miles to the nearest one." He added, "You have a bottle for the baby? Can he have warm milk?"

She didn't care about milk, warm, cold or otherwise. But as worried as she was about Trip, she was still responsible for his children and she could tell Colin was hungry. "There's a bottle in with the diapers, I'll get it."

By the time she got back to the kitchen, Eddie was pouring milk into a mug he took from a cupboard for Noelle, adding a dollop of chocolate sauce and stirring it in. Noelle took the mug with a grin and wore a brown mustache within seconds.

"No chocolate for the baby," Faith said. "And we'll have to let it cool."

"I didn't get his too warm," he said as he poured milk into the bottle.

Faith tested it on her wrist while Colin grabbed for it, kicking his plump legs and squealing with anticipation.

As she sat at a chair and gave him the bottle, Eddie set a mug in front of her. He sat down opposite her with a mug of his own. She took a sip. Noelle, who had finished her drink, was beginning to droop.

"Is your hot chocolate okay?" Eddie asked.

"Yes, thank you, fine." She took another swallow, anxious to get it down so Eddie would stop playing host and come up with a alternate plan.

He seemed to sense her anxiety. "Mama's car is in the garage. We hardly ever use it, but I keep it running. I can put chains on the tires and drive into Laxton."

"Or to the neighbor's house. It would be closer, right?"

"Sure."

"I could go," she said.

"It's an old car, Miss Bishop, and it might need nursing along in this weather. I'll go. If Mr. Tripper can trust me, you can, too."

"It's not that I don't trust you, Eddie, but so much time has passed, I'm worried we're going to be too late. Plus, maybe your mother would be uncomfortable with me and the kids in her home without you here, too."

"Mama isn't home," he said.

Faith blinked tired eyes a couple of times. "I thought she was disabled."

"She takes the bus into Shay every so often. They got a special hydraulic lift." He got to his feet. "You stay here, I'll go get the car ready."

"I'll help you," she said.

"It'll be faster if I do it alone. I'll hurry, I promise. Then we can all get in the car and drive into Laxton, okay?"

She nodded as he took a dry coat off the hook by the back door and left the house. A blast of cold air reminded Faith how miserable it was outside.

Meanwhile, Colin had fallen asleep with half the milk left in the bottle. Noelle's head tipped forward, her chin touching her chest. Faith got to her feet, her knees wobbly again. "Come on, Noelle, let's go into the parlor, we'll put our warm clothes on. We have to be ready to go."

She had to nearly drag Noelle back to the parlor, and once there, the little girl immediately climbed onto the sofa and collapsed against the cushions. Faith lay Colin on the other end. For a second she stared down at them, startled by how deeply they slept.

Alarm bells in the back of her brain rang with muted tones. Coats. Scarves. Mittens. She needed to find where she'd put them. By the door, maybe. As she turned away from the children, the room began to spin and she stumbled. A vague sense of alarm tugged on her brain. She found herself on her knees, then on her stomach, the pattern of the hooked rug a maze of swirling colors an inch from her nose.

And then she knew no more.

SHE AWOKE TO A familiar sound. The room was almost dark. She sat up, her head woozy, and hearing the sound again, turned to find Noelle crying in her sleep.

She crawled to the sofa and took Noelle's hand. "Sweetheart?" Faith's mouth felt dry. In fact, she felt almost like she had twelve hours earlier when she'd awoken in the hospital. "Noelle? Wake up."

The child's eyes didn't open. Faith shook her gently, but Noelle's head just rolled to the side and her eyes stayed shut. At least the cries stopped. Faith moved to Colin. The baby lay on his back, both arms flung open, so white he looked dead.

Time stopped. Her heart stopped. The world stopped.

And then she saw his chest rise and fall.

What was going on? Where was Eddie? What was taking so long?

Something was wrong. She slowly got to her feet, shaking her head, rubbing her eyes, knowing there was something she should be seeing but not sure what it was. She opened the front door and walked outside, almost falling down the stairs. It was cold and she hugged herself.

She wanted to yell Eddie's name, but yelling seemed impossible, so she whispered it. For some reason, that reminded her of Trip and her mind cleared a little. Trip. He was in danger. How long had it been? Was he still alive? Wouldn't she know if he was dead, wouldn't she feel it?

She stumbled across the yard. The barn was in front of her, the snowmobile in front of that. She bypassed the machine and opened a small door behind it.

"Eddie," she said. *He was doing something to his mother's car... That's right, they had to get to a phone.* He had to be in here somewhere.

There was a light on in the far corner. In the space between herself and that light, she saw an old car, and beside that, a beat-up truck. A third spot sat empty; presumably it usually held the truck Eddie drove to and from work.

She shook her head. *Think....*

She walked to the car and looked down at the

tires. Something about the tires. Chains! Eddie was fitting chains onto his mother's car.

But this car had two flat tires. It didn't look as though it had been driven in years. The windows were cracked, spiderwebs draped from the broken antenna to the hood.

Beside it, the old truck was fitted with snow tires. Maybe she had it wrong, maybe she was confused. Maybe Eddie was going to drive them all in the old truck. Only where was he… What was taking so long?

She looked around the barn, searching for him, walking vaguely toward the light at the back, rubbing her temples. Between the night before and this day, she was bruised and battered from stem to stern. There wasn't a place on her body that didn't hurt.

A sound finally infiltrated her consciousness. It sounded like Noelle crying. How did Noelle get out here? Faith whirled around and realized the sound came from the bench in the back, the one over which the lamp was suspended.

But there was nothing on the bench but a few tools and a white paper and a laundry marker. She picked up the paper. Names, all crossed off….

Leola Tripper

Susan Matthews

Gina Cooke

Marnie Pincer
Faith Bishop
Noelle Matthews

She choked back a startled cry as every hair on her body bristled, every corpuscle suddenly woke up.

Marnie's name had been inserted between Gina's name and Faith's name as though she was an afterthought. Whatever Eddie's plan was, it apparently included every woman on that list.

The beginnings of a terrible fear began to swell in her breast. Then she heard the noise again, the hopeless crying, and tilting the suspended light with the marker, angled it into the barn, searching. Its light fell across an old green tarp.

An old green tarp.

She released the shade. The light swinging back and forth cast dizzying arcs as she made her way to the tarp. This one wasn't rolled, thank heavens. Something underneath the tarp moved. Faith almost jumped out of her skin. She knelt slowly and with an unbelievable sense of dread, peeled back the tarp.

A woman in her late thirties wearing a pink-and-white uniform lay on the floor. A heavy rope circling her neck was tied to an eye bolt set in a cement block sunk into the ground. Another rope tied her wrists to her ankles, and though she made feeble mewing noises, she seemed to be unconscious.

A name tag on her shoulder read *Marnie*.

A voice from the door froze the blood in Faith's veins.

"Faith? Are you in there? Come on out now. It's almost your turn."

Eddie.

She looked around for a weapon.

"Faith? I'm standing between you and those kids. If you don't come right now, then I'm going to go get the baby. And I promise you, Faith, I'll kill him. He's not important, do you understand?"

Though Faith's head was clear, she understood nothing he said except the part about killing Colin. That he was capable of doing such a thing was obvious from the poor woman lying near death at Faith's side.

Leaving the tarp rolled back a little to make it easier for the comatose waitress to breathe, Faith stood up. She walked toward the door where she could see Eddie's round-shouldered frame high-lighted in the entry.

"What do you want?" she said.

Now she could see he held a handgun. As she made her way through the cluttered barn her mind raced. They'd been away from the ranch for hours. Trip, by now, was either dead or coming to get them. The children had one of two chances— either Trip got to them or she stopped Eddie.

Could she wrestle a gun away from a crazy man?
She could try.

She had to keep Eddie's mind off the kids until
Trip figured out where they were and came for
them. He could follow the tracks; he was trained,
he would get here.

If he was still alive.

"What do you want from me?" she asked again.

She was close enough now that he could reach
out and grab her arm, and he did this with unexpected vigor.

"What do I want?" he growled in her ear. "I want
Luke Tripper to lose every female he ever cared
about. I've killed his mother and sister and that
lovestruck babysitter. The waitress is almost dead
and you're next. Then the little girl."

"You pulled the plug on his mother," she whispered. "You started the fire that killed Trip's sister
and her husband."

"The husband was collateral damage, just like
the baby will be."

"But you didn't kill Gina right away, and
Marnie is still alive—"

"The babysitter was going to be my last, but she
tried to get away."

"So you killed her."

"It was time. I have to say, you've been harder
than the others. I was going to take you the day I

flattened your tires, but that bodybuilder got to you first, so I settled on the waitress. Then last night, that same bodybuilder got in the way again."

"You were the one my landlady thought was going to rent my apartment if I cleared it out."

His smile gave her the creeps. "There's no one to get in the way this time, little Faith. It's just you and me."

"And that mess at the ranch? You did that?"

"I just started the fire. My plan was to nab you while Mr. Hero put out the flames. That escaped felon coming along when he did was bad luck, but I turned it around, didn't I? I got both you and the little girl at the same time."

"Eddie, listen to me. Trip will find you—he'll know we're here."

"He thinks I took you the other direction," Eddie said.

"But he'll catch on. He'll suspect you, he'll figure it out—"

"Don't you get it," he said softly. "I don't care. I just want Luke Tripper to suffer."

"But why, Eddie?"

Her question brought tears to his eyes, tears that made glistening tracks down his doughy cheeks. His nose began to run and his plump lips crumbled. As childlike as he might appear, however, the cruel strength of his grip as he twisted her arm behind her back and pulled her outside was anything but innocent.

The snow had stopped, there was even the occasional glimpse of moonlight. Still it was cold. Faith hadn't put on a coat before leaving Eddie's house, but the frigid temperature wasn't what made her heart seize.

"Eddie, this is madness. We're friends. Noelle likes you. How can you even think of hurting her?"

"For my mother," he mumbled. "It's for Mama…." His voice was swallowed by a gulping sob. For a second his grip loosened as he ran his gun arm across his face.

Faith took the opportunity to wrench her arm from his grasp. Her action had the side benefit of knocking the gun out of his hand. It fell into the snow and in the dark she didn't dare take time to try to find it. She moved toward the house, but he quickly blocked her way, seeming to swell in size, twice as crazed as before.

Okay, if she couldn't get past him to the house, she would decoy him away from it. She turned and ran into the night.

His laugh echoed around her as she scampered into the overgrown maze of the Christmas trees. "You can't hide from me for long," he bellowed. "I know every square inch of this place. I'll find you."

"Come and get me," she gulped as she dodged prickly branches and plowed through the snow, knowing she was leaving a wake a blind man could follow. She had to get deep within the trees, down under the branches where there wasn't a lot of snow, and that meant she had to crawl on her belly.

Chapter Sixteen

The ranch swarmed with emergency vehicles. Red lights bounced off the snow as fire trucks finished dousing embers.

George Plum and another ranch hand were on their way to the hospital, Paul Avery and the man guarding the gate were dead, as was Gene Edwards. Neil Roberts had been blown into little pieces when he hid behind the truck and Trip shot the fuel tank.

The ranch house had suffered smoke damage, two barns were history, as were scattered outbuildings. Trip's leg was wrapped in bandages and the ambulance crew were waiting for him to get into their vehicle. They were in for a long wait because Trip wasn't going anywhere until he figured out where the hell Faith, Noelle and Colin were. He stood talking to Fire Chief Gallows and Sheriff Torrence—the FBI was still in transit.

"Eddie said he'd take them to the Peters place—

it's less than a mile away, our closest thing to a neighbor," Trip said.

"The Peters are the ones who called in the fire," Gallows remarked.

"I checked with them—my family didn't arrive. There must have been trouble between here and there."

"We have deputies out looking for them," Torrence reminded him.

Behind Trip, Buttercup whinnied and he looked up hopefully. It was one of the deputies, returning on snowshoes from the direction of the Peters place. Snowshoes, Trip had learned, were how Edwards and Roberts had managed to get to the ranch without being heard. They'd left their van outside the ranch, shot the guard at the gate and hiked in on snowshoes stolen from Edwards's dead uncle.

"Anything?" Trip asked anxiously.

"Nothing, sir. No tracks, no accident, no nothing."

Trip swore. "Where the hell did Eddie take them?"

"Who is this Eddie?" Gallows asked.

"Eddie Reed. The son of the woman on the bus, right, Trip?" Sheriff Torrence said.

Trip turned around slowly. "What are you talking about?"

"The woman on the bus, the one you couldn't get out in time. Eddie Reed is her son."

"Her name was Emily Dorsett."

"That's because Eddie was her son from a previous marriage. I thought you knew. When I heard you hired him, I just assumed."

"No, wait," Trip said, unable to make sense of this. "I went to Emily Dorsett's funeral."

"I know," Gallows said. "I saw you and your sister's picture in the newspaper."

"Yeah, Susan went with me, but I didn't see Eddie there."

"He was a lot heavier then. I bet he's dropped fifty, maybe sixty pounds since summer. Grew himself a mustache, too. I thought maybe he had a girlfriend."

"He was here after the fire that killed Susan and Sam, offered to help. Nice kid," the fire chief remarked.

"He and his Mom were tight," Torrence added. "He couldn't even bring himself to go to the grave-yard after her funeral. I think he spent most his life out on that Christmas tree farm, even though it went belly-up when his stepfather ran off."

Trip had stopped listening. Why hadn't Eddie told him who he was? Why had he kept it a secret? Why hadn't he mentioned being here after the fire?

"Maybe he took them to his house," Torrence

said. "He lives west of here, on the other side of the hill."

"You've got to get someone out there to look," Trip said, because his gut instincts were making leaps his head could barely keep up with. Eddie working across the street from where Gina's car was found abandoned. Eddie just happening to be there when Faith had four flat tires David Lee swore he didn't flatten. Eddie in the restaurant, his pale eyes taking in everything. Eddie showing up at the ranch the day Duke was arrested. For that matter, a "soft-spoken man" had called in Duke's DUI. Another "nice guy" had bought Duke all the liquor he could hold.

"Call Eddie's house," he said.

But there was no phone number, listed or unlisted, for Eddie Reed or his mother. Torrence, sensing Trip's growing concern, ordered his men to drive over to the Reed house and take a look. There was no Laxton police department.

Trip couldn't stand waiting a second longer. Anything was better than standing there, wondering.

He'd been lucky to recue Buttercup from the burning barn—no way a saddle had survived the fire, and he wasn't going to take time to go searching for one in the livestock barn. He grabbed a handful of mane and swung up on the gold horse's back, coming close to sliding off again when his injured leg struck the other side.

The EMTs both jumped to their feet. "Hey, Mister!"

"Trip, what the hell are you doing?" Torrence asked.

"Give me a flashlight," Trip demanded through a gasp of blinding pain. He checked his pockets for ammunition. He had extra.

"We'll take care of—"

"It's too windy for a helicopter. Your deputies have to go the long way around the hill... Maybe I'm wrong. Maybe Eddie is just a nice guy, maybe they had an accident on the way there, maybe they're all sitting around drinking a damn cup of cocoa. Whatever, I'm going to follow what's left of their trail and find out. Now give me a flashlight. Please."

Torrence took a xenon gas–filled flashlight off his belt and handed it up to Trip.

Trip nodded once and took off, rounding the house to the garden shed where Eddie had said he found a snowmobile. Sure enough, he could just make out the parallel tracks in the pale moonlight, leading away from the open shed. Leading west.

He leaned over Buttercup's neck. "Let's go, old girl."

THE OVERGROWN TREE FARM was a nightmare of branches. They caught in Faith's hair, tore her clothes, scratched her skin. Faith moved fast, trying only to bury herself inside all the trees so Eddie would have to work to find her. She had to keep him away from the house. She wouldn't even think about the possibility he'd forget about her and hurt Noelle. She was on the list for next. It was her turn.

Yeah, well, the first time he couldn't get you, he snatched Marnie Pincer.

But she couldn't allow herself to think like that because it would immobilize her. She had the gut feeling he would give chase and she had to stick by it.

A few minutes later, her gut feeling proved right as she heard the loud whine of the snowmobile. A bright light flashed over her head. She didn't know if Eddie caught sight of her ducking under a tree, only that the engine went off. She dug down in the snow and sharp pine needles, shaking so hard she was afraid her clattering teeth would give her away. Her clothes were wet from the snow, her hands and knees cold beyond endurance.

"I know you're around here somewhere, Faith."

She kept her face down, hoping her blue jeans and black sweater would camouflage her as she huddled under the lowest dark branches of the trees. Her blond hair was a concern, so she did her best to keep the wind from whipping it around her face. It had either started snowing again or the wind was knocking the snow out of the trees; either way, she hoped it hindered visibility.

As long as Eddie was talking to her, he wasn't hurting Noelle or Colin. *Come on, Trip. Figure it out.*

"You want to know why," Eddie said, and she could hear him tromping through the snow. It sounded as though he was whacking and prodding the overgrown trees with a machete. He seemed to be twenty or so feet away from her and she all but stopped breathing.

"Your boyfriend, Mr. Hero, killed my mother," Eddie said. He didn't seem to be crying anymore. "He left her on that bus to die."

His mother was the woman Trip hadn't been able to save, the woman he couldn't get out.

"She was the best woman in the world. Well, you saw the things she made. Rugs and dolls and pillows. Always busy, that was Mama. Knew her bible from start to finish."

And kept Eddie sane as long as she was alive...

"But Mr. Hero decided she wasn't worth saving," Eddie said, his voice bitter and ragged with exertion. "He got everyone else off that bus, even sinners and whores, but he left my mother to burn to death. He murdered her."

Maybe it was because Faith's head was pressed

so close to the earth that she detected another sound, coming fast, a rhythmic thumping, a sound she could almost place.

A horse running. She was hearing the pounding of horse hooves, and it was getting closer.

And then it stopped.

The lights flashed over her head again; Eddie was within ten feet of her. One more tree and he'd step on her hand. She closed her eyes lest the whites give her away. She tried to stop shaking.

"Hey, listen, I got a deal for you," Eddie said, veering off in the other direction. "How about you give yourself up and I don't kill the baby. It might be fun to have a baby."

She heard him slashing and whacking for a few minutes as she did her best to be as small and invisible as possible.

And then she heard another rustle in the trees, the sound of a branch cracking. Someone else was lurking out here and she knew who. It was Trip. He'd ridden a horse to the rescue. It had to be him. And Eddie was headed in his direction.

She had to do something to give Trip the time he needed. Could she still move or had she frozen to the ground? She tried flexing strained muscles and rolled from her hiding spot. Getting to her feet was a slow and painstaking process. Halfway there she said, "Eddie?" Her voice wasn't much more than a whisper, easily lost in the noise of the swaying trees. She tried again. "Eddie?"

The light immediately swerved her way, blinding her. Throwing her arm over her eyes, she yelled, "You win. I'll do what you want if you'll leave the children alone."

"Not the girl," Eddie said, advancing. "I have plans for the girl."

"Then the baby," Faith said. "You'll spare Colin?"

"Sure," he said, almost upon her. She gritted her teeth, more angry than afraid. Angry that his insanity had cost so many people their lives, that he could so calmly discuss killing Noelle.

Another cracking noise and Eddie turned quickly, his flashlight swinging with him. Had he heard Trip?

Was Trip even there, or was it just a manifestation of her wishful thinking?

Eddie's back was to her. Without giving it another thought, she bent at the waist and plowed into him. They both fell into the snow and his gun fired. He threw her around until he was on top of her. One hand still held the gun, the other tightened around her throat, fingers pressing into her soft flesh.

The unbearable pressure seemed to last an eternity and then she heard Trip's voice. "No, you don't," he yelled, and he must have pulled Eddie off her, because suddenly she could breathe.

Eddie started punching, the gun went off again, and then Eddie was running away, swallowed by the dark. "Stop him," Faith croaked as Trip reached down for her. "Trip, stop him, he's going for Noelle."

Trip immediately turned and gave chase.

After an eternity, she heard more gunfire, two or three shots, maybe more. When it was quiet, she found herself standing, listening. No matter who had or hadn't survived, she had to get back to the house, back to Noelle and Colin. She took a step and then he erupted from the dark, gripping her around the waist, pulling her against him.

"Oh, Trip."

"Are you okay? Can you walk? Oh, God, I thought I'd never see you again."

"I knew you would come if you could," she said, as he kissed her face a dozen times. "I knew it."

"You're freezing to death," he murmured, taking off his jacket and wrapping it around her. "Where are the children? Faith, where are they?"

"At his house. He drugged us. And Marnie, she's in the barn. I don't think she has much longer. Is Eddie—"

"Dead."

Supporting each other, they limped through the

trees toward the access road where the snowmobile, headlight still glowing, sat abandoned. It wasn't until Trip walked in front of the machine that she saw the bright red blood staining the bandage around his leg.

"You were shot."

"I'm okay." He looked around and added, "The gunfire must have scared off Buttercup."

"You rode to the rescue on Buttercup? A big, manly stud like you?"

"Don't tell anyone," he said. "Can you bear one more ride on the snowmobile?"

She never wanted to see it again. "Yes, if it's with you," she mumbled.

They climbed on and rode back to the house in time to see two deputy vehicles pull into the driveway. The deputies spied them at once and came forward.

"In the barn, near the workbench at the back, a woman, under a tarp," Faith said. "She needs an ambulance fast."

One deputy immediately took off to the barn, radio in hand, making the necessary calls. The other said, "Ma'am, sir, you both look as though you could use an ambulance, too."

"We're okay, but there are children inside who've been drugged."

"And there's a body out in the trees," Trip said.

He grabbed Faith's hand. She acted as his crutch as he haltingly, but with determination, made his way up the front steps and across the porch.

The house was as quiet and still as a time capsule. Under the lights, she finally got a good look at Trip and he at her, and they both smiled in recognition of their sorry states.

"Over here," Faith said, her numb feet tingling as she walked. When she caught sight of the children sleeping exactly as she'd left them, she expelled a breath she hadn't even known she was holding.

How could she ever have abandoned two small children alone in this house? She vaguely recalled her own confusion, but it was like trying to remember the details of a dream. At the time, going to find Eddie had seemed the logical thing to do, but in retrospect…

She was closest to Colin, so she picked him up gently, relieved when he made little faces and sounds. As Trip hefted Noelle in his strong arms, the small doll Eddie had given her fell from her hand. They both stared at it for a minute before Trip kicked it under the sofa.

"I think the best thing for us to do is keep them inside where it's warm until the ambulance arrives," Trip said, kissing Noelle's forehead.

"I agree."

He gazed at both children with such tenderness Faith's throat closed. "There's a lot I'm just beginning to understand."

Did he know Eddie killed his mother and sister? Had he figured out that he himself was at the center of the violence, that as nonsensical as it was, Eddie had blamed Trip for his mother's death?

Eventually he would have to know all this, but not now. "Me, too," she said.

"You were remarkable out there," he added as he sat down, still cradling Noelle, groaning when her limp body pressed against his leg.

Faith sat down next to him, pulling a blanket free and covering the children—and him. He looked as though he needed a hospital bed far worse than the kids, but she knew he wouldn't taken care of himself until they were taken care of first. That's the kind of man he was.

As for herself? The truth was, she might be banged up and exhausted, but she also felt alive in a way she hadn't for a long time. "You were the remarkable one," she told Trip.

He kissed her gently. "You must be psychic," he whispered, his gaze caressing her.

"Me?"

"You told me I would fall in love someday with a fearless woman. You predicted it. And I have."

She started to protest. Her, fearless? That was

crazy talk—and yet, that's exactly how she'd felt when she'd gotten to her feet and engaged Eddie in conversation, when she'd tackled him to give Trip the time he needed. She'd been too angry to be afraid, too worried about the people she loved to stay hidden.

Fearless.

As the distant sound of sirens reached her ears, she leaned against his muscular shoulder and stared up into his eyes.

"Luke Tripper, will you marry me?"

The look in his eyes was all the answer she needed.

Epilogue

"They're here!"

Noelle came rushing inside, almost knocking over Colin.

Faith caught Colin before he landed on his head and followed Noelle outside. The July day was warm, with just a touch of a breeze—a perfect day for an outdoor wedding.

Colin wiggled free when he spied the four little girls tottering toward him. Faith's nieces, Brianna, Antoinette, Jillian and Juliet, were fourteen months old now. They all had identical brown curls and pink cheeks, were all dressed in fluttery yellow dresses, and all adored Noelle, who, also dressed in yellow with her brown hair curled for the event, looked enough like them to be their older sister.

Colin, chubby and blond, a dead ringer for his deceased father, laughed and clapped his hands as he charged into their midst. He loved girls.

Faith stopped and kissed each wiggly little girl before making it to her best friend and sister-in-law, Olivia. "I'm so glad you came," Faith said.

"We wouldn't miss this day for the world," Olivia whispered.

"Where's the groom?" Zac asked as he folded her in a brotherly hug.

"Sheriff Torrence called him about a robbery—he'll be out in a minute. How about Juliet and Dad? Are they far behind you?"

"No. They'll be here in a half hour or so."

At that moment, Trip opened the front door and came outside. The white shirt he wore with his jeans set off his tan, making him so handsome Faith felt weak in the knees. He'd taken over for Chief Novak after the chief botched the murder investigation back at Christmas. Trip's contentment with being back in law enforcement, even at a local level, glowed in his eyes.

When he got close enough, he opened both arms and whistled at Faith, who was wearing a white shirt and jeans, too, as she planned on riding Buttercup to the altar. "My God, woman, you look good enough to marry," he said.

She laughed as she threw herself into his arms.

"Ms. Faith?"

This came from George Plum who had been around back with some of the ranch hands getting the barbecue ready to go. "You get around to signing those invoices yet?"

"Give the boss a day off, George, she's getting married!" Trip said with a laugh.

That's what Faith was. The boss. She'd taken formal leave of teaching after the last term and signed aboard as the new boss at the Triple T. She had found over the past few months that ranching might not be in Trip's blood, but somehow it was in hers; and besides, she wanted to be at home with the children. With her children.

"I signed them this morning," she said. "Listen, did Hal get down to look over the fences we talked about?"

"Not yet. I figured I'd send him tomorrow while you guys are off on your honeymoon…."

"George, go away," Trip interrupted with a laugh. "And you, young lady, don't you know brides are supposed to forget about work on their wedding day?" With this, he swept her into his arms. She threw back her head and laughed.

Her wedding day.

The rattle of the cattle guard announced another vehicle. Trip put her back on her feet as a van appeared around the bend.

"Your first guest?" Olivia asked.

"Yes and no," Faith said, smiling up at Trip. Arm and arm, they walked to the van as Nate and

Marnie Pincer got out. "Where do we set up?" Marnie asked.

"This is so nice of you guys to cater our reception," Faith said, taking the waitress-turned-caterer's hands.

"Nice?" Nate scoffed. "If it weren't for you two, I wouldn't have a wife, our boy wouldn't have a mother."

"Don't mind Nate, he gets mushy at weddings," Marnie said, but she cast him a warm look as she said it.

"George, come help the Pincers," Trip said, putting an arm around Faith.

As children and adults chattered around them, they looked at each other, building an island of peace in a sea of commotion. Later, when they were truly alone, she would give him the news there was going to be another baby at the Triple T.

But not yet.

There was plenty of time.

* * * * *

*Celebrate 60 years of pure reading pleasure
with Harlequin®!*

To commemorate the event, Silhouette
Special Edition invites you to Ashley
O'Ballivan's bed-and-breakfast in the small
town of Stone Creek. The beautiful innkeeper
will have her hands full caring for her old
flame Jack McCall. He's on the run and recovering from a mysterious illness, but that
won't stop him from trying to win Ashley
back.

*Enjoy an exclusive glimpse of
Linda Lael Miller's
AT HOME IN STONE CREEK.
Available in November 2009
from Silhouette Special Edition®.*

The helicopter swung abruptly sideways in a dizzying arch, setting Jack McCall's fever-ravaged brain spinning.

His friend's voice sounded tinny, coming through the earphones. "You belong in a hospital," he said. "Not some backwater bed-and-breakfast."

All Jack really knew about the virus raging through his system was that it wasn't contagious, and there was no known treatment for it besides a lot of rest and quiet. "I don't like hospitals," he responded, hoping he sounded like his normal self. "They're full of sick people."

Vince Griffin chuckled but it was a dry sound, rough at the edges. "What's in Stone Creek, Arizona?" he asked. "Besides a whole lot of nothin'?"

Ashley O'Ballivan was in Stone Creek, and she was a whole lot of somethin', but Jack had neither the strength nor the inclination to explain. After the way he'd ducked out six months before, he didn't expect a welcome, knew he didn't deserve one. But Ashley, being Ashley, would take him in whatever her misgivings.

He had to get to Ashley; he'd be all right.

He closed his eyes, letting the fever swallow him.

There was no telling how much time had passed when he became aware of the chopper blades slowing overhead. Dimly, he saw the private ambulance waiting on the airfield outside of Stone Creek; it seemed that twilight had descended.

Jack sighed with relief. His clothes felt clammy against his flesh. His teeth began to chatter as two figures unloaded a gurney from the back of the ambulance and waited for the blades to stop.

"Great," Vince remarked, unsnapping his seat belt. "Those two look like volunteers, not real EMTs."

The chopper bounced sickeningly on its runners, and Vince, with a shake of his head, pushed open his door and jumped to the ground, head down.

Jack waited, wondering if he'd be able to stand on his own. After fumbling unsuccessfully with the buckle on his seat belt, he decided not.

When it was safe the EMTs approached, following Vince, who opened Jack's door.

His old friend Tanner Quinn stepped around Vince, his grin not quite reaching his eyes.

"You look like hell warmed over," he told Jack cheerfully.

"Since when are you an EMT?" Jack retorted.

Tanner reached in, wedged a shoulder under Jack's right arm and hauled him out of the chopper. His knees immediately buckled, and Vince stepped up, supporting him on the other side.

"In a place like Stone Creek," Tanner replied, "everybody helps out."

They reached the wheeled gurney, and Jack found himself on his back.

Tanner and the second man strapped him down, a process that brought back a few bad memories.

"Is there even a hospital in this place?" Vince asked irritably from somewhere in the night.

"There's a pretty good clinic over in Indian Rock," Tanner answered easily, "and it isn't far to Flagstaff." He paused to help his buddy hoist Jack and the gurney into the back of the ambulance. "You're in good hands, Jack. My wife is the best veterinarian in the state."

Jack laughed raggedly at that.

Vince muttered a curse.

Tanner climbed into the back beside him, perched on some kind of fold-down seat. The other man shut the doors.

"You in any pain?" Tanner said as his partner climbed into the driver's seat and started the engine.

"No." Jack looked up at his oldest and closest friend and wished he'd listened to Vince. Ever since he'd come down with the virus—a week after snatching a five-year-old girl back from her non-custodial parent, a small-time Colombian drug dealer— he hadn't been able to think about anyone or anything but Ashley. When he *could* think, anyway.

Now, in one of the first clearheaded moments he'd experienced since checking himself out of Bethesda the day before, he realized he might be making a major mistake. Not by facing Ashley— he owed her that much and a lot more. No, he could be putting her in danger, putting Tanner and his daughter and his pregnant wife in danger, too.

"I shouldn't have come here," he said, keeping his voice low.

Tanner shook his head, his jaw clamped down hard as though he was irritated by Jack's statement.

"This is where you belong," Tanner insisted. "If you'd had sense enough to know that six months ago, old buddy, when you bailed on Ashley without so much as a fare-thee-well, you wouldn't be in this mess."

Ashley. The name had run through his mind a million times in those six months, but hearing somebody say it out loud was like having a fist close around his insides and squeeze hard.

Jack couldn't speak.

Tanner didn't press for further conversation.

The ambulance bumped over country roads, finally hitting smooth blacktop.

"Here we are," Tanner said. "Ashley's place."

* * * * *

Will Jack be able to patch things up with Ashley,
or will his past put the woman he loves
in harm's way?
Find out in
AT HOME IN STONE CREEK
by Linda Lael Miller.
Available November 2009
from Silhouette Special Edition®.

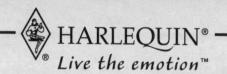

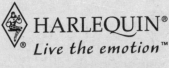

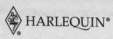

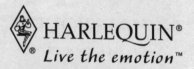

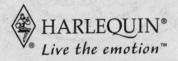

Harlequin® Historical
Historical Romantic Adventure!

*Imagine a time of chivalrous
knights and unconventional ladies,
roguish rakes and impetuous
heiresses, rugged cowboys
and spirited frontierswomen—
these rich and vivid tales will
capture your imagination!*

*Harlequin Historical . . .
they're too good to miss!*

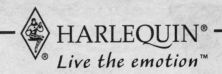

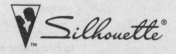